Sunday's Colt
and Other Stories of the Old West

Other Boson Books by Randy D. Smith

Bohanin's Last Days
Dodge City
Fort Larned
Heroes of the Santa Fe Trail: 1821-1900
Hunting Modern South Africa with Powder and Ball
Lovell's Prize
Scott City
The Devil's Staircase
The Red River Ring

SUNDAY'S COLT

and Other Stories of the Old West

by

Randy D. Smith

BOSON BOOKS
Raleigh

Published by **Boson Books**
An imprint of **C&M Online Media Inc.**

ISBN 978-0-917990-92-2

For information contact
C&M Online Media Inc.
3905 Meadow Field Lane
Raleigh, NC 27606
Tel: (919) 233-8164
e-mail: cm@cmonline.com
URL: http://www.bosonbooks.com

Designed by JoEllen Lowry

Contents

Ty Lee Driscoll and Red River Sam Go A-Mavericking
or
One of Twenty Years Running Iron and Busting Ponies in Texas Comanche Country

Ty Lee Driscoll and Red River Sam Bonnet decided that they were tired of working for wages and set out for the Mesquite Canyon country with six of their best dogs to catch some cimarrones. Old Dil Townsen was never much to work for anyhow, so Ty Lee and Sam figured if they were going to risk life and limb chasing wild cattle through the mesquite and thorns for two bits a head they might as well be doing it on their own for two dollars. There were plenty of Longhorns still prowling the brush country south of San Antonio free for the taking and the markets in New Orleans were high. Some said a man could get six dollars Yankee gold for good cattle and the boys figured they could have a couple of hundred head there in three months. That was more money than them old boys had seen since they came to Texas during the war—certainly more than they would ever even smell working for that scrawny swindler, Townsen. Any man who begrudged good maverickers extra flour and coffee after they branded a hundred head from only two weeks work was nothing more than a skinflint and potential horse cutter. They were the best there was at catching cimarrone—bar none. Let Old Dil just try to replace them. He'd learn the value of an extra pound of coffee and three-pound sack of flour for hardworking wranglers with the best catch dogs in Texas. Nothing more need be said on the matter.

Ty Lee was a tall, lanky drink of water with about half his teeth gone, a hawk nose and eyes so hollow they looked like they belonged on a strangled cat. His night horse was a knock-kneed grulla mustang gelding with all four legs black from the fetlocks down. He called that bronc Fester, but nobody could figure where he came up with such a handle. Old Fester was a good one and could see in the dark better than any ten other broomtails a man could assemble. Ty Lee had a new Mother Hubbard saddle that he paid fifteen dollars for in Austin. He was partial to wearing red and brown plaid wool pants with the legs stuffed down stovepipe black army boots and always sported a pair of ten-pointed Mexican spurs. He wore an old broad-brimmed brown felt hat so loose and floppy that he had to sew up the front of the brim to the crown with rawhide thongs to keep it from blowing down and blinding him in a hard cow chase. He carried a '51 Navy Colt in a cross-draw holster and packed a Zouave carbine in his saddle boot that he liberated off a dead Yankee just after Yellow Tavern. His shirt was so threadbare and ragged that most gents wondered why he wore it at all. His elbows were plum tan from exposure as he had worn clear through both his long johns and linsey woolsey shirt long before the spring green-up. But he was a goer, could like to paint the sky yellow with a lasso, and the best damned night herder in Texas.

Red River Sam Bonnet was the more sedate and showy of the partners. He was every bit as skinny as Ty Lee but didn't ride like a sack of bones rolling down a railroad grade. He also took more pride in his appearance. Although his mustache hadn't been trimmed in months and draped over his bottom lip like an old horse blanket on a fence rail, he did own a whalebone hair comb and used it every morning that he could. He liked to part his hair down the middle like a town dandy and herd the excess locks over and behind his ears. If he kept his hat on tight his hair tended to stay in place, so he usually had his tie-down string drawn tight against his chin. He was fond of wearing a fancy fireman's red wool bib shirt and gold silk scarf that he claimed was given him by a sporting lady named Naomi, more famously called Sugar Lil around Houston. He packed a finely tuned Confederate dragoon .44 six shooter and Rio Grande camp knife. They were carried in a matching star concho-decorated loop holster and sheath. Sam was the brains of the outfit, but that didn't say much. Generally, he had a broad plan for the day devised before Ty Lee finished his breakfast coffee, and Ty Lee wasn't much to challenge authority or argue trivialities as long as whatever they were doing was from the back of a horse or rail of a bar.

The boys had been saddle pards for over two years and rode for Townsen most of that time. They had their own string of six ponies and some fine mongrel catch dogs bred mainly from a bluetick bitch and whatever came along when she was in heat. They raised them from pups and sold the bitches when they had some cow sense trained into them. Now that the old bitch had passed on, they ran four roan brothers, and a couple of brindle hounds of no relation. They called them Tobe, Rye, Musket, Flowers, Stinky, and No-Good, with No-Good being the best of the pack. He was a lop-eared, scarred-muzzle blue like his momma with a put-out left eye and a disposition reasonably akin to a rabid wolf. But he was hell in the thickets and unafraid of any beast on two, four, or six legs. If a man could quirt him bad enough he minded most of the time, but nobody, man nor dog, turned his back on him if he was on the prod. He may have looked like sin, but his teeth were good and he knew how to use them. Both men usually quirted him with a revolver in the other hand just in case he took it upon himself to go for the nose or throat like he did a fighting bull. Musket was probably the second best dog because he was easier to handle, a good brawler, and regularly brought in game. The boys couldn't remember how many snakes, armadillos, and rabbits Musket had shared for the campfire. He had developed a taste for rats of late and the boys weren't up to sharing, even though they appreciated the gesture. The other problem with Musket was that he might take it upon himself to go hunting right in the middle of a wild cow catch if something scared up. But since No-Good liked fighting better than eating, the other dogs usually hung it out with him. Generally it worked out for the best if a man could beat No-Good badly enough to settle him down after the cattle were lassoed.

They located a thick stand of cedars along a creek and set up a maverick camp. They built themselves a crude lacco to keep their fleabags dry and a rambling cedarwood holding corral set through the creek channel. The first night out they managed to flush thirty head of mossbacks, yearling calves, and young bulls. They decided on a left-hip running iron brand they labeled the Rafter-I. It was easy to slap on and they hadn't seen anything similar in the country. They also dewlapped the left ear. Neither man was unhappy with the look of the cattle they brought in. For a bunch of wild linebacks, they weren't so thin that the sun shined through them in the dawn light, and only one old cow was footsore.

The pickings were better than the Williamson county country where Townsen had settled, and after working four miles or so of canyon ambushes, they had seventy-five head corralled and branded in the first seven days with only four headshot to keep their ponies from being gutted. They kept huge mill fires burning each night around the corrals to fence break the new stock. They guessed that some of the three-year-olds would probably weigh out at six hundred pounds. Both agreed that there were several bunches they had missed and if their luck and the corral held, they could put together at least a herd of a hundred or so before breaking camp.

That was about the situation when they had their first bad break and lost No-Good. They were making a late evening sweep when Musket flushed a varmint leading No-Good and Stinky into some rocky hills above a dry slough. The boys didn't see the flush but could tell they had something up when Musket went to baying on the scent. They didn't think too much of it until the bays turned to cries and yelps. It was so bad that Ty Lee figured they had a mountain cat or bad boar cornered and were getting cut to ribbons. He lit out after them to shoot whatever it was before one of them was ruined.

The rocks were so steep that he had to tie up his pony and climb the face on foot. Just to be safe, he checked the loads in his Colt and hobbled his gelding. He had to climb several hundred yards into the hills before he came upon the awful sight. He found No-Good rolling in the dirt and wiping his muzzle with his forepaws, yelping like he had turpentine painted on his crap hole. He was riddled with porcupine quills from the top of his head to the bottom of his neck. Being No-Good, he had waded right in for first blood and had taken the brunt of the quills. Musket and Stinky were perforated with quills as well, but nowhere near as seriously as No-Good. They were baying at the base of a black oak with a boar porcupine perched quietly in the first fork. Angry that his dogs could have been ruined, Ty Lee pulled his Navy without thinking and blew that porcupine right out of his perch, whereupon the dogs set to him again only to take on more quills. Ty Lee had to quirt them both back from the corpse before they were blinded as well.

Old No-Good had only one good eye to spare and that porcupine did his work on it. It was already turning gray with poison. He was a miserable beast and Ty Lee knew there was no hope of saving his sight. He pulled his Navy again and sent No-Good to hell where he was sure the devil would find good use for him gnawing on some Yankee carpetbagger's ass. The boys spent the rest of the night by the campfire jerking quills from the other dogs. By morning, both dogs were sick, but they managed to shake the poison and were as good as new within the week.

Sam figured it was a bad sign and said they needed to get their seventy-five head started for New Orleans. He was tired of taking chances with the scrawny beasts they were finding when he had good cattle already branded and ready to break trail. He figured they could pick up a few more along the way. Besides, with No-Good dead and two other dogs sick, that was all the cattle two wranglers could probably handle through the hardwoods and swamps. So, they saddled up and started the herd for the coast, hoping to trail break the herd in the open before the trees closed in.

They pushed the cattle hard for twenty-four hours to keep them worn down until they settled in. Right off they realized they had a bad bunch of runners. A mosshorned, linebacked blue cow settled in at the lead, but she was skittish and had that wild-eyed look common to a lobo that had never known anything but thicket and brush, choya and cactus. She had a raggedy-ass, bloat-bellied, red-roan, bull calf on the teat that was just as crazy as she was. They set off at a near lope and never backed off the lead for two days. It was all the boys could do to keep the drag brought up tight. Sam tried to maintain the point, but wore out a pony every four hours just keeping her and her homely whelp held back. Ty Lee and the dogs were kept busy on the drag and wing, keeping the rest within sight. When they made camp on the second night, they had to mill the herd for an hour before it settled. It was then that the boys decided to turn for Rockport and see if they could find a buyer assembling a herd for New Orleans. There wasn't a prayer of holding this bunch together once they hit the swamps and boggy bayous without hiring some more cowboys, and risking wage money they didn't have.

They fought that mob of Longhorns for the next two days wondering what that old mosshorn cow would pull next. She'd jump two feet to clear a stick no bigger than a garter snake, shy at the song of a meadowlark, and balk at a foot-wide spring. She hooked anything that came between her and that calf. When they did reach a fair-sized river, she jumped in and began swimming for the far shore before the others could even drink. The only reason the boys didn't shoot her was for the hope that if she would eventually settle, they'd have a fine leader and could loaf the rest of the way into Rockport.

About mid-morning they spied three old boys waiting for them as they came out of a stand of locust. The leader was a rough-looking lout riding a glass-eyed, scrawny bay. He had a Burnside carbine resting across his lap and a Colt Navy perched high in a cross draw holster. The other two were just common raggedy-ass hands packing rusty Colts and looking more like grub line riders than anything a good outfit would hire on. The leader held up his hand, like he was the law or something, for the boys to hold up their cattle. The problem was that once the mossback cow had set her mind to make for the next line of underbrush, she was the deuces to stop.

While Sam tried to work them into a mill, those three just sat there on their ponies like they were of independent means. Sam decided right then and there that if they weren't the sort to lend a hand when they were the ones calling the halt that they were probably scalawags or outcast Missouri Redlegs. When Ty Lee and the dogs finally brought up the dregs and the remuda, Sam turned his pony to face them.

"Where you boys going with them cattle?" the lout asked.

Sam was in no mood to palaver and decided to be abrupt. "Going to shit after the hogs eat 'em," he said.

The lout didn't particularly like the comment. "You know whose range you're on?" he said with the grim look of a guy with a new grown hemorrhoid.

"Since when is this closed range?" Sam asked before spitting a wad of tobacco at the glass eye's forefeet.

"You're on Dunham range," the lout said.

"Who's Dunham? You?" Sam shot back.

"We ride for him."

Sam gave out the expression of a gent who had just blundered on a well-used outhouse.

"You some kind of a gun outfit?"

"We protect our cattle and our range."

"If you can manage to move that crowbait more than six feet and take a look at them cattle you'll notice right quick that they have a Rafter-I road brand. They sure don't have any other brands."

"Where'd you get them?" the lout asked.

"Ain't none of your affair. They was mavericks and now they're carrying a road brand. That's the end of it." Sam figured these three for herd cutters and looked over his shoulder to see what Ty Lee was up to in case he needed him.

Ty Lee was just leaning on his saddle horn, smiling, scratching, and watching like a freshly paid hooker looking through a sweet shop window. The pack gathered round his pony like old saddle pards and waited for their orders. Sam knew that whenever Ty Lee smiled like that he was ready to fracas when given the word.

"We're a-gonna need a toll for crossing our range," the lout pronounced. He acted pious enough to be some Baptist sky pilot on a soul-saving visit to a Methodist divorcee.

Sam shook his head. "We ain't a-gonna do it."

The lout puffed up like a horny toad. "The hell you won't. Me and the boys will see to that."

Sam grinned coldly. "You got help? You're gonna need help."

The lout frowned and spoke quietly...kind of growly-like. "You're about to find out."

"Sic 'em!" Ty Lee spit under his breath.

Old Musket must have been feeling guilty about leading No-Good to his grave because he lit into that scrawny bay with everything he could muster. Stinky and Flowers waded in just as hard as soon as they figured out what "sic 'em" meant. Not to be outdone, Tobe and Rye made for the other two.

That old glass eye jumped about four feet to starboard and went to bucking. The lout only stayed with him for the first foot, and then he gave everyone a demonstration on how to break a fall with your face. The whole area turned into a dusty haze of bucking horses, cursing cowboys, swirling dogs, and flying saddle rigging. It wasn't a minute before all three of them herd cutters were ground bound with their ponies headed for the high lonesome—snorting, farting, and kicking at the pursuing pack.

The old mossback took it as her cue to charge through and she led the herd and remuda for the far thickets at a dead run.

"Let's go!" Sam yelled as he dug his spurs into his roan and pointed him toward Longhorn tails and pony leavings.

"What about these fellers?" Ty Lee called in confusion.

"To hell with those fellers!" Sam's voice faded as he charged away.

One of the other two, a feisty, bandy-legged little drip with an Irish goatee, drew his Colt and tried to cock it with both thumbs. The damn thing was so rusty that the flat spring snapped with a pop. All he could do was curse and throw it at Ty Lee as he trotted by. He couldn't have missed him worse if old Aunt Suzy had been throwing an anvil at a roadrunner.

Ty Lee just shook his head with disdain and dug in his spurs. He left them there choking on his pony's dust cloud.

That old mossback had finally risen to her potential, for she had all seventy-five of them linebacks in a full-blown stampede. They hit those thickets with a crash, a shudder, and a bang, scattering like quail along a dry wash. The wash was thirty feet wide and eight feet deep at the banks. When the mossback hit the bank she gave a wild-eyed leap like she actually believed she could fly to the far side in a single bound. She must have taken landing lessons from the lout because she came down square in the middle headfirst, dug those long horns into the sandy bottom, and snapped her miserable old neck like a twig.

The others musta thought she was giving lessons because about half of them tried the same stunt with varying degrees of success. Suffice it to say, none of them made the far bank, first try. Those that hadn't broke something or busted a gut came to their feet and scrambled up the far bank like they had someplace to go. The other half took to fighting brambles and dodging tree limbs until they figured where the leaders were going and followed forthwith. After they crawled up the other bank they ran for Canada and a high rocky slope in between.

By this time the dog pack had given up on pony chasing and was scrambling in pursuit. Only Rye stopped long enough to sniff the mossback and decide she was dead before lighting out after the herd.

Sam drew up his pony and gazed down on the death and destruction of the wash. He counted three with broken legs, one busted-gut cow kicking in the dust, and the strange display of a blue-roan mossback in the middle, tail in the air, dead. Worst of all, old Fester wasn't far from the others nursing a broken foreleg, just a-standing there in the sand and his distress.

Sam eased his broomtail down the bank and drew his dragoon. He shot Fester first, and then worked his way through the others putting them out of their misery. When he got to the mossback he studied her for a moment, sorry he had an empty gun. He would have liked to have put one into her just for being like she was and leading Fester to his ruin.

Ty Lee watched silently from the bank. "Thanks for putting Fester out of his misery," he said softly.

Sam nodded without looking up. "I know he was your horse and I didn't have the right but I just couldn't stand to watch it."

"That's the way of it. I'd a-thought old Fester coulda seen better than that. He'd a-never crossed that wash in the dark. We're gonna be a pony short now, and a good un," Ty Lee said.

Sam shook his head and sighed. "Naw, I saw two of them herd cutters' nags running with the stock. We'll trade them even up, saddles and all, for Fester."

Ty Lee nodded and started his pony down the bank. "Sounds good. We need to ride afore them Longhorns scatter in the breeze."

Sam drew up his pony's head and gently spurred. "Good enough."

Both pronounced it a near miracle that the herd had stayed together as well as it had. By the time they had them rounded up, they were only ten head short, including the four littering the dry wash, and a net gain of one pony. Rather than waste time and possible reprisals from the herd cutters, they pushed on. By the next day the strays had caught up and rejoined the herd. Longhorns are like that.

It went to raining the next day and continued solid for a week. The boys got so waterlogged that their ears started leaking. They spent several shivering nights in the saddle just keeping the herd milling, and dry firewood became so scarce that they ran cold camps three nights running. They came to a wash almost identical to the massacre site, but this time it was running bank-full. Longhorns that the week before would have balked crossing a piss trace bailed right in and tried to swim for the far bank. The current swept and scattered them for close to a mile. When they crawled up the other bank ten more head were gone, probably food for the catfish. It all happened so fast that the boys didn't have time to consider their options. It was a major loss, however, and they could see their profits dwindling.

They came to a gentle lowland meadow running along the Nueces River in Live Oak County. They stopped there and dried themselves out for a spell, letting them Longhorns belly down on the lush floodplain grass. Sam observed that it would be a fine place for a couple of fellows to run a two-loop outfit. They weren't getting any younger and it was time to think about settling down. They could build a little cabin on the rise, get out the running iron, and maverick up a fine herd in no time. If they played their cards right they could find themselves a couple of lonely señoritas and have a fine life. Ty Lee didn't say much but it was plain to see that he wasn't opposed to the idea, especially the part about the señoritas. Of course, he was tired and easily swayed.

A week later they drove a thoroughly trail broke herd of sixty Longhorns into Rockport and headed straight for the pens. They were out of flour and beans and hadn't even had a hot cup of coffee in four days. They were so bad off that Ty Lee was talking of buying a new shirt with his share of the profits.

A heavyset fellow with a peg leg stepped from the pen office to greet them. "You're late," he said with a smile.

"Late for what?" Sam asked without dismounting.

"The packets have already sailed. I don't look for another cow market for four months."

"Well, we still got cattle for sale. What's the market?"

"I suppose we could buy them for the hides and tallow and make out. I'd go fifty cents a head."

"Fifty cents! What kind of a price is that? I heard they was selling for six dollars in New Orleans."

"They was bringing four dollars here six weeks ago. But the market is played out for now. In six months it'll be up again. If I was you boys I'd grass them up and come back in April."

Sam turned to his disgusted partner. "What do you think?"

"I ain't gonna sell for fifty cents. We coulda done almost that well working for that skinflint, Townsen."

Sam spit and then thought for a while. "What about that meadow we stopped at back in Live Oak County? We could winter them there and build the herd. We been talking about starting our own herd. Some of these old girls are with calf. What do you think of that?"

"I want some coffee and flour. I ain't about to winter it out without some coffee and flour."

"We could sell one of them cutter's nags. It ought to bring ten dollars or so. We could do that?"

Ty Lee was sullen. "I need another shirt."

Sam nodded. "We both do. We'll get ourselves a couple of shirts to boot. What do you say, partner?"

Ty Lee thought for a moment. He thought so hard he almost forgot what it was he was considering. He nodded acceptance rather than have to hear Sam explain it again. They sold a horse, bought the supplies, and turned the herd back for the Nueces.

They found that meadow again and built themselves a dugout along the floodplain. They even took time enough to build a wood shingled roof, a couple of rope cots, and a horse pen. They allowed those Longhorns to scatter along the river and went to mavericking up some more. They grew so fond of the place that they decided to head to Live Oak and register their brand.

The County Clerk's face turned a bright red when the boys told him their brand. "Are you boys trying to make some kind of joke?"

Sam shook his head. "Ain't no kind of joke. We want to register the Rafter-I as our brand. We built us a place and we got some cattle scattered all along that river."

"I hate to tell you boys this, but the Rafter-I is Hopper and Wade's brand. They run the largest outfit in this county. I figure you just scattered your cattle in with about four thousand others with the same brand."

Sam's mouth dropped and he felt sick to his stomach.

"I guess we could go back and rebrand them," Ty Lee said.

The county clerk shook his head. "I wouldn't advise that, boys. Hooper and Wade are running some of the best gun hands in this part of Texas. Hell, they hung four Mexicans just last week for stealing branded cattle. The way I figure it…if you like your skins…I'd just write those cattle off and decide on another brand."

Sam shook his head. "Forget it. We'll mosey." He led Ty Lee out of the building into the square.

The boys sat on a low stone fence surrounding the courthouse square and waited to get up the gumption to ride home. It was a plum discouraging turn of fate and they were having difficulty dealing.

A buggy came down the street and stopped in front of them. Neither looked up. Old Dil Towsen leaned out of the buggy. "Hey, what you boys doing in Live Oak? I've been looking for you all over creation."

Sam looked up and smiled. At that point he was glad to see any familiar face, even if it did belong to an old horse cutter. "Howdy, Dil. What are you doing here?"

"Going to Rockport to line up some spring buyers. I've got a good-sized herd to bring in. I sure could use you boys if you're willing."

"We're sorta running an outfit of our own," Sam said without looking up.

"If you'll excuse me for saying so, Sam, you boys don't look too prosperous. You could trail in my cattle and mix in your own cows for nothing. I'd pay you wages and let yours go for the same lot price. Now, what could be fairer than that?"

Ty Lee looked up and frowned. "I'd expect plenty of coffee and flour."

Dil nodded ashamedly. "I'm real sorry about that, Ty Lee. I've felt real bad about that incident ever since it happened. I shouldn't have treated you boys that way. I'll never short grub you boys again. You have my word. What do ya say?"

They went to work for Dil that winter and nothing more was said on the matter. Ty Lee took along an extra stash of coffee and flour, just in case.

Ty Lee Driscoll and Red River Sam Go to Abilene

Old Dil Townsen decided that if he was ever going to have a pot to piss in he needed to find a better market for his cattle than south Texas. He'd heard stories that the railroad was pushing into Kansas and the Yankees were paying seven times the going price for linebacks than he could get in Williamson County. That made Old Dil's mouth water since he reckoned he had nearly five thousand head scattered through the hills and thickets. He ordered his wranglers to bring in some full-grown steers and figured he'd risk sending a few up to Missouri to see if he could turn a dollar. Nobody in the outfit had ever been to Missouri or Kansas so he hired a gent named Tyco Reeves to help blaze a trail to Sedalia or wherever he could find a market. Tyco was an experienced hand and drove Texas Longhorns east throughout the war to keep Bedford Forest and that fool, Braxton Bragg, supplied with meat for their troops.

Tyco was a tall redhead with a bushy beard and blue eyes so pale they glowed in the morning sun. He was a sure enough reb managing his business with a withered left arm and half his left foot gone from bullet wounds he received when he tried to run the blockade at Vicksburg. He knew how to trail cattle for long distances with a minimum of loss and the word was that Tyco could tell a man to "go to hell" and convince him he was overdue leaving without hurting his feelings or his pride…a born trail boss.

Old Dil knew Tyco's reputation but just to be on the safe side he sent two top hands along to keep an eye on his interests. Those old boys were Ty Lee Driscoll and Red River Sam Bonnet. Perhaps you've heard of them? They were the gents that slapped the brand on the original Murder steer and rode down the Black Queen when everyone else said that black would never be ridden by any pietistic mortal.

Ty Lee Driscoll—his mother preferred his Christian name, Ty Lee—was a raggedy-ass, hawk-faced, nearly toothless drudge who looked and dressed like he had just been paroled from Andersonville prison after an expense cut. His pants were so loose fitting that he took to wearing an extra belt just to keep track of where they were under the folds of his shirt. He favored a moth-eaten grulla gelding from his pony string that he tagged Fester II, but nobody could figure how he came up with such a handle. He ate, slept, and rode with a motley pack of half-starved, flea-bitten, snake-eating, bluetick crosses that would just as soon bite a man as look at him. His hat was a fright, his boots a joke, he smelled like sin, and his shirt was an embarrassment in mixed company, but he was about the best Texas vaquero there ever was and anybody with a good eye could tell it.

His partner, Red River Sam, was getting on in years to be a wrangler. Some said he was nearly forty, but he cowboyed almost as well as Ty Lee and he knew all his letters and sums. Being an educated man he was more philosophical and prone to expound on the theories of cattle breeding, horse breaking, and biscuit making. He was Christian enough to take kindly to saying the words and leading a good hymn or two when a friend, or stranger for that matter, needed putting under. His prize possession was a gold silk bandanna given him by Sugar Lil O'Brien herself, better known as the Arkansas Darling when she worked the troops in Little Rock. He had a broad nose that looked like it had been riddled with buckshot and during the high shine of the day his appearance was that of a mustache wearing a broad brimmed sombrero and a red fireman's shirt. Generally, he kept his hat low and his opinions to himself to all except Ty Lee. They were solid saddle pals and their word was as good as a Philadelphia bank note.

Even Old Dil was surprised when the boys cut out seventeen hundred steers from three to seven years old. Some of the older beasts probably weighed in at seven hundred pounds or so. They slapped on an H7-T road brand and pointed them north. Other than Ty Lee and Sam, the other six cowboys were all youngsters fresh off the sugar teat and raring for the high life. To keep the crew happy, Dil sent his prize thirty-dollar-a-month cook, an ex-slave named Candle Corn, to manage the supply wagon and fix the vittles. Those were the days before anyone had ever heard or even dreamed of a fancy Studebaker chuck wagon.

Candle could make melt-in-the-mouth corn bread that was too princely for sopping up pinto beans and fat back. Most of the crew ate it like cake and preferred it to about anything a man could shove on a tin plate. No cook in Texas could slap together a more larapin apple pie or sandhill plumb cobbler. He could heat up a boiling pot of coffee quicker than any man alive and always had a fresh biscuit handy for a belly treat.

Candle's only drawback was that he was so damned ugly. He had whiplash scars on the back of his neck and side of his face the size of a lariat end and a white right eye from one of his beatings that never seemed to track with the good one. Word was that he was a Mississippi cotton slave managed by a white trash field master who took a shine to his mamma. When Candle caught the overseer taking his pleasures with her down by the creek, he laid hands on him and was nearly lashed into the next world for his trouble. He ran off a couple of times and received worse whippings after the bloodhounds ran him down. They even trimmed the toes of his right foot with a hatchet to slow him down some but it failed to slacken Candle's determination to be a free man. When he finally did manage to make a getaway, he came to Texas and went to work for Townsen. By that time Mississippi was in smoldering ruins and nobody bothered to check him out. Candle didn't carry a side arm, but he packed a bone-handled butcher knife Indian fashion along the small of his back. No wrangler in his right mind went up against Candle when his temper was up and he had that knife in his hand. That twelve-inch blade fare-thee-well lived there when it wasn't in its sheath.

Little Billy Nix was the remuda wrangler and all of thirteen summers old. Like most of Townsen's crew he was a throw-away who rode shirtless and barefoot into the ranch on a bareback mule with nothing but a tote sack and worn out harmonica. Old Dil took a shine to the orphan and put him on as Candle's "Cook's Mary." In a couple of years he was in the saddle and learning the trade from Ty Lee and Red River. He was on his way to being a first-class wrangler and all the boys thought the sun sat in his pants. He was never too proud to shirk nor never too meek to take shit off of anybody. The other boys knew he was a favorite and gave Billy a wide berth. It was also to their credit to be associated with such a goer and top broncobuster even if he wasn't more than seven stone soaking wet.

Those steers trailed out about as good as any bunch of Longhorns could manage. They stampeded only once during a lightning and hail storm in the Indian Territory and seemed to get fatter as they made their way north. Tyco knew just the pace to keep them eating steady and traveling smoothly. The pickings on the trail were a heap better than any of that scrub brush in Williamson County and Tyco made sure that they got every blade he could muster along the way. Other than the ten head of stragglers they paid the Shawnee to cross their land and a couple of drop deads, they kept their losses to a minimum. With the unbranded stray cows and calves that joined up with them on the trail, they crossed the Kansas line with almost break even numbers.

They turned east toward Sedalia after Tyco felt they were past the threat of border ruffians. Not ten miles later they ran into a cowboy riding out to inform the Texas herds that the railroad had pushed west to a new settlement called Abilene in Kansas. From the rider's directions and some flyers from his saddlebags, Tyco figured he could cut almost two hundred miles off the trip if he drove for Abilene and made the risky decision to take the man's word that the place was for real and wasn't part of a swindle. Twenty days later they milled the herd seven miles south of a single ragged line of unpainted frame buildings, a few tents and a fine set of railroad loading pens called Abilene. They were the third and smallest herd in, so they had to wait their turn for the buyers to make a bid. Tyco rode into town to make the arrangements and the boys lined up for Candle to get out his mixing bowl and give them a fresh haircut.

One gent, a feminine fat loafer from Kansas City named Orrie Gates, offered them fifteen dollars a head for the steers, but they had to take his note for payment. Ty Lee and Red River would have nothing to do with the offer and came close to having it out with Tyco over the matter. Since the cattle weren't made out of paper, the boys figured they should have something other than paper for a settlement. When the loafer took offense and said that his note was as good as gold in Kansas City, Red River countered by saying that Kansas City paper was good for only one thing in Texas and he would look him up when he was ready to have a movement. Two days later the loafer returned with an offer of twelve dollars a head in notes and coin. Sam studied the paper carefully and although it looked genuine enough, he sent him packing. By this time Tyco was getting plum disagreeable, but the boys stuck to their guns. Horse cutter that Old Dil was, he deserved better than paper and the boys would settle for nothing less than gold or silver coins. They had a bunkhouse papered with Confederate currency and didn't trust that Union script one bit better.

The next day a buyer from Richards and McDuffy, Indianapolis, Indiana, showed up in a buckboard carrying a strong box. He bid the whole herd, counted out $18,700 in gold coin, and told the boys to take it or leave it. The boys took it and agreed to deliver the herd to the stock pens the next day. Tyco went along with the deal but was indignant, arguing that they'd lost $6,800 in profits through sheer ignorance. The herd was delivered, the crew paid its wages, and Tyco put the remaining bags of money in the town bank's new safe.

As Tyco, Ty Lee, and Red River stepped from the bank, Tyco handed the deposit slip to Sam and asked when the boys were going to deliver the money back to Dil. As far as he was concerned they were quits and he was riding on to greener pastures. The boys nodded and Ty Lee told Tyco to make sure the barn door didn't hit him in the ass as he left town. There was a tense moment or two before Tyco chose to walk away. He was tough as a bootheel but when it came to facing Ty Lee Driscoll, even Tyco knew his limitations.

As Tyco drifted down the street, Sam turned to Ty Lee. "Well, partner, we got us purt-near eighty-five dollars apiece. What's your pleasure?"

Ty Lee smiled broadly. "A shave, a store-bought bath, and a new outfit, top to bottom."

Red River gave him a surprised look. "I figured you'd want a drink or something."

Ty Lee watched the whelps from the crew making their way to the Wish-Key bar and shook his head. "Nope, I'm done with such doings. I want me a new first-class outfit and I don't want to stink it up first day. We can get ourselves a steak and a beer later."

Red River smiled. "All right, partner, let's head for the general store and see what they got."

Billy Nix was following the same plan when the boys entered the Willam Gage Merchantile and Sundries. The sprout was standing in front of the mirror carefully studying whether his new Stetson looked better on him cocked to the left or to the right. He smiled when he realized the boys were watching him. "First thing I've ever owned that didn't belong to somebody else first."

Ty Lee nodded. "Buy the best, boy. It may be a spell before you'll be able to replace it."

Billy smiled broadly and looked back at the mirror to admire his hat. "I intend to."

Ty Lee picked out new long johns, a dark blue bib front shirt, tan breeches, and a pair of knee-high brown boots with a white Texas five-pointed star on the shin of each. He took nearly a half-hour deciding on a hat. Finally, he went with a Stetson as well. He gulped hard when the clerk asked for $30.00 payment. "A month's wages," he mumbled.

Sam chose another red shirt, this time with dark blue piping along the collar, bib, and cuffs. He went to a dark outfit, choosing black pants, black boots, and a new black Stetson of the same low-crowned, broad-brimmed style as the others. When the clerk offered him a selection of scarves, Sam smiled and pointed to the dog-eared gold bandanna around his neck. "No, thanks, I'm partial."

They carried their new clothes to the barbershop and lined up for their baths. An hour later the three of them walked confidently from the shop looking like clean-shaven, freshly washed, first-class Texas wranglers.

Red River was surprised at just how slim Ty Lee was when he wore clothes that fit. "Damn, Ty Lee. We better feed you something before you disappear," he said. "What about you, Billy? Or are you wanting to belly up with the others?"

"If it's just the same to you fellows, I just as soon have me a big steak, too. We just don't want to forget to get Candle a bottle for camp. He wants a drink and these here Abilene fellows said they didn't want no nigger stinking up the street."

Ty Lee nodded. "We'll get a couple of bottles and do our drinking with Candle back at camp. Hell, there ain't a Yankee storekeeper in this town that's a patch on Candle's ass."

Billy nodded and grinned. "That's for sure."

"Ain't it funny?" Red River observed with a taciturn smile. "Them Yankees was perfectly willing to die for a nigger's freedom but now that he's got it, they got their carpetbagger noses higher in the air than ever. Don't make sense, does it?"

"There's a lot about that war that never made sense," Ty Lee answered. "I'll bet ya one thing. Most of them up-turned noses belong to gents who didn't have the gumption to pack a rifle-musket for blue or gray. If they had, they'd be talking different about the likes of Candle Corn."

Red River and Billy looked at him oddly. It was the first time they'd ever heard old Ty Lee say something profound or for that matter, very intelligent.

"You suppose it's the change of clothes?" Red River asked Billy.

Billy just shook his head in mystification.

They strode over to an eating house called Trail's End Café and settled down at a table next to the window so they could watch the street doings as they ate their dinner. All three ordered a tall beer, a thick steak, fried potatoes, and watermelon preserve pie. As they were settling into their grub, a thin-framed little gal in a purple velvet dress walked through the door and sat alone at a table next to the wall. Ty Lee, who seldom bothered much with the female persuasion, took an immediate shine to her. He placed his fork on the table and silently stared at her as she gave her order to the waiter.

After a while Billy noticed Ty Lee's preoccupation and nudged Red River under the table with his toe. He motioned Red River's attention to Ty Lee with a crafty glance. Red River turned in his chair to see what Ty Lee was studying.

That little gal was all of five feet tall and couldn't have weighed more than eighty-five pounds. She possessed a sad countenance and looked ahead through dark expressionless eyes. She had a narrow nose with a gentle bump on the bridge like those classic beauties in the mail order catalog and sat in an erect almost rigid position, her backbone never touching the back of the chair. Her dark brunette hair was lifted gently from the base of her delicate neck into a precisely crafted bun. Her complexion was light but her skin glowed healthy. She had a fragile, willowy air about her—feminine, soft, porcelain. She weren't no raving beauty at first glance but drew an increasing appreciation with study. After a while a fellow wondered why he hadn't noticed her beauty before, sort of like red hills laced with dark green buffalo grass and cedars in the spring. It was always there if a fellow just took the time to appreciate it and once he did, he never forgot it. She was that type of woman.

Red River gave Billy a wink before turning to Ty Lee. "Why don't you go over there and say something to her?"

Ty Lee looked down at his food. "Naw, she wouldn't take no truck with the likes of me. She'd probably call the law and pronounce me a masher in right quick order."

"A fellow never can tell. Sometimes them little gals like the attention. Hell, Ty Lee, you ain't looked or smelled this good for years. Now's the time. You need to strike while the iron is hot."

Ty Lee cut a harsh course with his eyes as he spoke softly. "I ain't something a pretty little gal like that would be interested in. I reckon she's got a beau due any minute. Afore I knew it, some city slicker'd have a six shooter stuck in my ribs."

"I could ask her for ya," Billy said in earnest.

Ty Lee puffed up like an Arkansas cottonmouth. "Don't you even presume that I need the likes of you to do my introducings for me. Boy, you got clabber for brains and that's fer sure."

Red River could see that Ty Lee was having a difficulty pressing on his nerves. The joke was over and a gent never pushed a saddle pard beyond his limit...if he had any sense of right. "We need to be finding us a couple of bottles anyhow. Let's finish these steaks and be on with it."

Ty Lee nodded and returned to his steak. Billy looked at the table and quit his meal. Ty Lee had never talked to him that way and his feelings were hurt. Ty Lee and Red River's opinions were just about the most important elements in Billy's life and even mild disapproval from either cut deep into the orphan's insides.

Ty Lee sighed, quit his steak as well, and shook his head. "I shouldn't have said that. I'm right proud of you, boy. I just let my saddle get set crooked and tried to blame you. I'm apologizing fer that."

Billy smiled weakly. "Don't pay no mind. I weren't trying to spur you but I guess I did."

"It's women," Ty Lee said after a moment of uncomfortable silence. "Fair for a fact, nothing is more perplexing than what a gal can do to a man's reason. Steer clear of them all—that's my motto."

Billy looked up and smiled broadly. "Yeah, women. That's fer sure."

Red River winked at the boy. "That's fer sure." He went back to his steak in earnest.

It was then that the miracle occurred. That little gal turned toward Ty Lee and smiled broadly. Her teeth were as straight and bright as a piano keyboard. "Excuse me, do either of you gentlemen have the time?"

Ty Lee gulped hard. His eyes grew wide and his chin dropped to his shirt collar. "I—I reckon I don't ma'am. I never had much use for a timepiece."

Sam leaned across the table toward Ty Lee. "There's a clock on the wall behind her."

Ty Lee didn't seem to hear. He couldn't draw his eyes off her.

"Tell her the time from the wall clock, Ty Lee," Sam tried again.

Ty Lee shook out of his daze and meekly motioned toward the wall. "There's a clock just behind you, ma'am."

She turned and giggled. "My, I am such a fool. I did not notice it. How silly of me!"

"Yes, ma'am," Ty Lee stammered. "I mean...I don't think you're a fool or anything. I really hadn't noticed it myself."

She turned back toward Ty Lee. "I guess my companion is not going to make it." She sighed and shook her head in mock consternation. "Looks like I'm going to have to dine alone."

Sam was as quick on the uptake as a mustang finding an open corral gate. "Let's go, Billy."

"What fer?" the sprout asked, his voice rising. "I ain't had my dessert."

Sam eyes near to cut the kid's hat from his head. "We need to be a-getting that bottle for Candle."

Billy reacted like he'd just caught himself in the ear with his own quirt. "Oh, yeah, right. We need to be going, Ty Lee."

Sam wanted to slap the sprout out of his chair. "Ty Lee don't need to go. I'm sure he'd rather stay here and visit with the lady."

"You gonna stay here, Ty Lee?" Billy asked.

Ty Lee didn't take his eyes off her. "Yeah. You fellers go on. I'll catch up by and by."

"How you know where we'll be?"

Sam put his hand on Billy's shoulder and dug his thumb into his collarbone like he was spurring the Black Queen. "Let's go. Time's a-wastin'. Ty Lee knows our plans."

Billy winced from the pain, looked up at Sam and started to complain. He held up when he read Sam's face, then took on the look of a dunce in the corner who finally understood the lesson. He nodded meekly, feeling stupid for not getting the drift in the first place. "Yeah, we got to be going," he said in a too loud voice. "I don't think Ty Lee needs to go."

"Yeah. You fellers go on. I'll catch up by and by," Ty Lee repeated, looking like a freshly weaned calf watching his momma leaving for the range.

Sam near to jerked the sprout out of his bootheels. He threw down his money and roughly escorted the boy through the door. When they hit the boardwalk he turned for the Wish-Key. "I tell you, boy. You are about as slow as a turtle on a log in the middle of winter."

Billy shook his head. "How was I to know you was setting him up? How was I to know that she was really interested in him?"

"She was interested, believe me. Ain't no gal ever ask a perfect stranger fer the time unless she's eager to palaver. She was giving him the moon-eyed look and boy, when a gal like that gives someone like Ty Lee the moon-eyed look, it's the chance of a lifetime. You'll know that when you get some learning bout the feminine persuasion."

Billy nodded and struggled to keep up with his friend's pace. They made for the bar in quickstep, leaving their compadre to his fate.

Ty Lee waited until they were out of sight before he spoke to her. "My name's Ty Lee Driscoll. I ride for the H Bar Seven out of Williamson County, Texas."

She was impressed. "From Texas! Well, I'll declare. I'm Lannie Anderson. I work here in Abilene."

"Schoolteacher, I suppose," Ty Lee said.

She smiled prettily. "No, Mr. Driscoll. I'm a professional woman, although I've always wondered if I wouldn't make a good teacher."

"I reckon you would." Ty Lee smiled shyly and his face turned crimson.

She smiled at his bashful ways. "Your friends were certainly eager to be on their way. I'm glad you decided to stay for a spell."

Ty Lee nodded. "They don't need me."

She took one more small bite and daintily dabbed the corners of her mouth with her napkin. "That was a fine dinner and certainly first-rate company from an exceptional gentleman."

Ty Lee rose from his chair. "Thank you, ma'am. I guess I need to be getting on."

"I wonder if I might impose upon you one more time?" she asked.

He nodded and smiled.

"It is getting dark outside and with my companion's failure to keep our dinner date, I was wondering if you would be willing to act as my escort to my boarding house. I know it's asking a lot, but a lady shouldn't be seen unescorted this time of night."

"It would be my pleasure, ma'am. I'd be honored to escort you."

She stood and smiled sweetly. "Spoken like a true gentleman of the South."

He offered her his arm and proudly led her to the door...after leaving a silver dollar for her meal at his insistence.

***

Red River and Billy were just starting through the entrance of the Wish-Key when the doors sprang open from the other side and a flying body landed hard in the street and rolled through the dust and horse leavings toward the center. An instant later a six-foot wrangler with a full black beard burst through waving a Navy Colt in his right hand. "Ain't no hombre gonna crawfish on a bet with Gil Matters. You'll pay up, by God, or I'll send you to hell with Lincoln!"

Red River brushed Billy back against the wall with a sweep of his hand and forced the lad back to a safer position.

As Matters stepped into the street the doors sprang open again and cowboys filled the boardwalk to watch the action.

The gent in the dust slowly rose to his feet and silently brushed the grime from his suit. As he rose, Red River recognized him as the Kansas City buyer, Orrie Gates.

"Shouldn't we do something?" Billy asked quietly. "That fellow ain't hardly a match for that big guy in a tussle."

Red River shook his head. "No, sprout. It ain't none of our affair and I got me a feeling that Mr. Colt is going to even the odds right quick-like."

Billy's eyes went wide as he turned back to the street. "No kidding?"

"That big gent is so drunk I doubt he can hit a bull in the ass with a single tree," Red River said. "But, old Gates there, he's sober as a judge and wise enough to know he can't whip this feller. When the shooting starts, keep your head low."

"I said pay up, gott damn it," Matters cursed as he staggered a few steps forward and waved the un-cocked revolver before him.

Gates flung back his coat, drew a short-barreled Army from his belt and threw a shot wildly into Matters's right foot.

Matters yowled like a cat caught under a rocking chair and sent a shot toward the moon as he fell butt first into the street.

Gates threw another shot into the dirt next to Matter's holster, then stepped back as Matters cursed again and carefully aimed his revolver at the buyer's nose. A second later the shot sounded and Gates's eyes went wide as he realized that it was a clean miss and he was unharmed.

Gates made for a horse trough on the far side of the street. As he retreated, Matters studied the hole in his boot for a while before standing.

As the shooting angle changed, the crowd scattered to get well out of the line of fire. Red River grabbed Billy by the shirt collar and made a quick retreat around the corner into the alley.

A bullet followed shortly and the corner exploded into splinters.

Billy examined the hole carefully with his finger before Red River pulled him back. "Get your head down! This ain't over yet."

Matters hopped forward on one foot and sent two more rounds into the horse trough. Each round was returned by Gates as he crouched behind the trough and threw his shots wildly toward Matters without looking to see if he was hitting anything.

Then there was silence. Both combatants had emptied their guns. The boardwalk cowboys realized that it was safe to rush Matters and put an end to the affair before any more buildings got shot up. No less than five of them overwhelmed and forced him to the ground. Gates stood dumbly, his face as pale as a sheet, the smoking Army limply held in his hand. He turned meekly, dropped his revolver and threw up his dinner on the far boardwalk.

The law arrived and settled the matter in short order. Matters was carried to the doctor's office and Gates was tossed unceremoniously into the town jail—an oversized windowless outhouse with a chain and padlock holding the door fast.

After the street settled and the stories were told, Red River and Billy bought their bottles and rode back to camp. They spent the rest of the night telling Candle of the fracas, drinking whisky, and waiting for Ty

Lee. It was Billy's first encounter with Red Eye and he paid a heavy price in the morning. The lad was so sick that he wondered if he had to get better just to die.

It was mid-morning when Ty Lee rode into camp, filled his coffee cup and squatted by the fire. He didn't volunteer any news and no one asked. He just sat by the fire and stared silently into the coals.

After a while, Red River decided to make his move. "What do you think, partner? We better get into town and start that money back to Townsen."

Ty Lee nodded. "Fair for a fact. It's time to head for home."

As they saddled fresh horses, Red River said, "We probably ought to buy ourselves some grub for the ride back. Is there anything you need from the store?"

Ty Lee nodded without looking up. "I could use some tobaccy, but I'll have to get a loan from you."

"You spent it all?" Red River asked.

Ty Lee smiled and tightened his cinch. "She stole it. When I woke up this morning she was gone and my whole poke with her."

"The hell you say. We better get to the law and get them on her."

Ty Lee threw down his stirrup and lifted his foot into it. "No, let her have it."

Red River swung into his saddle and settled into the cantle. "That's a lot of money for one night, partner."

Ty Lee smiled and gently spurred his pony forward. "All I know is…for a spell there last night I was more than I ever was and more than I'll probably ever be." He turned to his partner and his eyes cut deep. "What's that worth to fellows like you and me?"

Red River gave it some thought, nodded, and rode on in silence.

The Black Queen

It was down near Trace Madres where riders from the Square Bit trapped her among thirty other head of mustangs. Those old boys had been trailing that bunch of broomtails for nearly a week when they found them watering in a shallow Comanche mudhole at the upper end of Blanco Cliffs Canyon. They closed off the exit with a thorny locust barricade and figured they would manage a right handsome remuda once the culls were shot and the rough rode out of the rest. At the time she was nothing more than a scrawny little black filly weighing less than six hundred pounds. In fact there wasn't much showy about her at all. She was block-headed, split-hoofed, knock-kneed, and sported a notched left ear. She had an inch-wide irregular scar running from the point of her nose to just below her right eye and her wild mustang mane looked like a drunkard's mop after a three-week binge. She was pure Spanish from her slit nostrils and narrow eyes down to her bushy fetlocks and ratted tail. Showy, hell! She was pretty damned plain when you think on it. About the only good to her was that she was free for the taking and could turn a man a four-dollar profit if he didn't break his neck riding the green out of her.

Her first victim was a Mexican named Banuelos. As was the custom, each vaquero roped out a choice in turn and worked his way down until the whole bunch had been green broke. Banuelos had just rode down a pinto buckskin for his fourth bronc and the pickings were getting pretty slim. It's told that he missed his loop on a scrawny gray and picked the black because there wasn't much difference between poor or a little poorer and he was getting tired. Anyway, she piled his ass in four jumps and then put a hoof through his forehead for his trouble. No one thought too much about it as that's the way it goes sometimes if a hand doesn't land on the run when he gets pitched.

Banuelos had a compadre by the handle of Mexican José. José took it upon himself to take retribution on the black the next morning. He lasted the same four jumps and hit the ground crawling. She broke his leg and bit off a piece of his shoulder before the others dragged him to safety. The Square Bit boys realized right quick that she was a stomping, teeth-gnashing, kicking, farting whore from hell with no mercy toward Mex, black, or white. Every man but Arky Blue had a go at riding her and she managed to get a piece of every one of them before he made it to safety.

Old Arky was nearing forty and said the hell with it after watching a few of the others. He figured that he wasn't up to spending another winter with a broken leg or arm and he had nothing to prove.

In fact, Old Arky was getting ready to put a .36 ball in her brain when he came up with the notion that the black might be the most valuable bronco of the bunch. He'd never seen any animal with less looks and more guts. When the boys got to considering it, not a man among them had lasted more than four jumps. Arky proposed that they might turn a nice profit by placing out wagers that no man could ride her. Of course they knew that there never was a horse that couldn't be rode, but if they kept a poke back to pay off the winner, they could turn a handsome profit watching the wannabes pay to get their turn at a dance with Satan's mistress. The way she went through the Square Bit crew it could be quite a spell before she was rode down, and the profits promised handsome. They came up with the name Black Queen for her, more to get a sucker's curiosity up than any other logic. A black queen is considered bad luck by many who favor the pasteboards and is an omen of impending disaster. Them old boys didn't realize at the time just how prophetic a handle they had placed on her.

Well, the Square Bit boys had no idea what a gold mine they had on their hands. The boys decided that since they had to work, they would make Arky the mare's manager. He quit work and took her out on circuit, hitting every small settlement, ranch house, and bar he could find. No less than forty wranglers, some of the biggest reputations in Texas, took a crack at her. In six months she piled all forty, killed two, and crippled a big-eared kid from down by San Antonio. She turned a five hundred dollar profit for the partnership. As she built her reputation, Arky made sure that she ate better than any broomtail alive and she gained a good two hundred pounds of green bile meanness. As she filled out, her strength grew but her quickness never slackened a bit. She grew into the strongest, meanest, quickest bitch that ever drew a breath or lipped grain from a trough. She had some kind of hate festering deep down in her guts for anything that walked on two legs. It weren't enough that she would just pile an hombre. She took a particular delight in leaving her mark on him before he could make a getaway. Once she felt the load shift from her back she took a specific satisfaction in turning on the rider with teeth snapping and hooves stomping in an ears-laid-back endeavor to finish him off with a murder. Some mighty fine vaqueros were witnessed with the wide-eyed shakes after making an escape. More than once old Arky had to pull his revolver to keep a gent from putting a bullet in her out of sheer frustration and hatred.

While the mare didn't change much during this time other than get meaner and stronger, Arky Blue did. Arky got the big head for better want of a term. He took to dressing up in fancy duds and standing the house to a drink when he entered any new establishment. He smoked nickel cigars, wore fancy stitched stovepipe boots and charged it all to expenses. While his pards labored away on the Square Bit, Arky led the high life and looked down on most folks as "unworthy" of his company. He'd twist his mouth and say "Well, sir, I'll tell you," like he knew something special and had some kind of privileged insight on just about any subject you cared to mention. When a wrangler took a pile from the Black Queen, he developed a particularly nasty inclination of ridiculing his efforts in spite of the fact that he never mustered the nerve to try her himself. As bad as most hombres hated the Black Queen, they held an even lower opinion of Arky Blue. This circumstance only encouraged more to try to ride the black down and consequently increased Arky's profits even further. In this case two wrongs made a right, as it boosted the cash flow significantly for Arky. He was one unpopular son of a harlot and had the money to prove it.

After cleaning house in Houston, Arky wandered down Williamson County way to see if he could find any new blood that hadn't heard of the Black Queen. The mare's fame was so great that several local outfits knew he was working their way. Rather than run the risk of being picked off one by one, the outfits decided to back one broncobuster and put all their money behind him. They wanted to break Arky and put an end to the Black Queen once and for all. More importantly they wanted a Williamson County rider to do it.

The hombre they picked was Rattlesnake Jack Calendar of the Olive-O. Rattlesnake Jack was more than just a broncobuster; he had the reputation of being an authentic gut-busting horse killer. He was a medium height, thickset scalawag with arm muscles that looked like they belonged on most fellows' legs. He had black, evil eyes deeply set under heavy bushy brows that joined in a single line across his forehead. He had the wide mouth and square jaw of a Cheyenne warrior and the bad humor to match. He didn't just break a horse if he lost his temper; he broke it down. Rattlesnake Jack wasn't satisfied with wearing a mount to a stall. If the animal riled him he'd go to spurring and quirting it until the beast went down beneath him. A lot of outfits would have nothing to do with him as a broncobuster because he ruined almost as many mustangs as he broke, but in this particular case the outfits reasoned that the best way to deal with a man-hater like the Black Queen was with a bona fide horse killer like Rattlesnake Jack.

Word was out and the cowboys were waiting when Arky Blue led the Black Queen into town. Hell, one feller remarked that it shoulda been a rustler's heyday with nearly every wrangler and outrider within a fifty mile area gathered in the Bale-O-Cotton Saloon for Arky Blue to step through the door. Arky knew that something was afoul when he recognized every hitch post on the street jam-packed with ponies. He tied his horses to the porch pole, swaggered through the swinging doors, pulled out a roll of bills, and stood the house to a drink. It took nearly fifteen minutes for the round to be poured, and the wranglers waited in near dead silence for Arky to make his announcement.

When every glass was filled, Arky raised his and toasted Jeff Davis, A. P. Hill, and the Confederate cause forever. No one could take offense at that and the wranglers were honor bound to join him with a fair hoo-rah for Texas. When they were finished Arky waited for the room to go silent before he started his handiwork. He swaggered to the center of the room, threw back his chest, and bawled out the words like he was speaking to a company of retired artillerymen.

"Well, gents, I'll tell you, I've got this little black mare outside. She just followed me into town as gentle as a hound dog. Well, gents, this here little mare needs to be ridden. She needs to be taught some manners. I told a feller I was a-going down to Williamson County to see if I could find someone to green break her for me. Gents, do you know what that feller said? He laughed out loud...right in the streets of Houston for every town dandy to hear...in front of the Bell of Texas Saloon...and said that there wasn't a Williamson County wrangler living that could ride that mare down."

He paused and gave every man a squint-eyed look of disdain.

"You know what I said? I said that there was plenty of fellows in Williamson County that could ride that mare."

He paused again and toothed an evil grin.

"Well, gents, that fellow just laughed again and said that he had five hundred dollars to risk against any five hundred dollars in Williamson County that there wasn't one lily-livered little reb scalawag alive or risen from the grave in Williamson County that could ride that mare down. Now, what do you boys think of that?"

A local rancher by the handle of Dil Townsen, owner of the H-7, stepped from the bar. It had been prearranged by all that Dil would act as the spokesman for the pool. "That little black mare out there—the one you say is just as gentle as a hound dog—that little black mare wouldn't be the Black Queen, would it?"

Arky Blue twisted his face into a caught-with-the-pie contortion and stuck his thumbs into the lapels of his fancy gold vest. "Well, sir, I'll tell you, I guess it would. Thank you kindly for asking. It keeps me from committing a possible misrepresentation."

"Just how many men has that gentle-as-a-hound-dog critter killed and maimed in the last six months?"

"Forty's tried to ride her," Arky grinned and cast a sly eye around the room. "To my best recollection she's only killed two."

"We hear she's killed four and sent one home to his mamma without legs that work."

Arky nodded and poured himself another drink. "Well, sir, I'll tell you. You said in the last six months. I told you the straight story cause them other two was nearly eight months ago. I honestly don't know if that other fellow can walk or not. You know how stories get started. But now, fellows, what's that got to do with the likes of Williamson County riders? Ain't it a bunch of you fellows that fought the good fight at Vicksburg? Men like that oughtn't be bothered by a few bad falls." He scanned the room slowly and grinned. "Or is the fight plum wrung out of Williamson County and carpetbagger courage all that's left?"

Some of the wranglers became uneasy and shifted their weight in their chairs. Townsen was their spokesman but this Arky Blue was getting himself right close to a lynching if he kept talking like that.

Arky could see that he was a-getting them going. Red necks and swollen eyes began protruding throughout the room. Still, he could tell he needed to tone things down a bit. "Now, I don't want you fellows to take offense. I was just asking a fair question. I'm sure no one in Texas doubts Williamson County courage."

Townsen smiled. "You talk a good war, but are you really up to fighting it?"

"What do you mean by that?" Arky asked softly.

"Five hundred dollars at even odds don't hardly seem fair for a man who rides down the Black Queen."

"What were you thinking?"

Townsen grinned broadly. "Eight hundred dollars at two-to-one seems more like it. I mean after you rode all the way down here, I wouldn't think it would be worth your time to see her rode for less."

"And you think you got a man that can ride her, do ya?"

"We do."

"Fetch him out so I can take a look at him."

Dil motioned for Rattlesnake Jack to come forward. Jack stepped to the fore and stood for Arky's inspection.

"Well, now, I'll tell you, this is one right handsome hombre. I can tell he's a vaquero through and through." Arky stepped to Jack's back and took a long inspection. "Straight as an arrow. Strong. Real strong. Just look at them shoulders. Them sharpened rowel spurs got horse killer written all over them. You boys wouldn't be a-trying to put a ringer on me, would you?"

Dil answered. "No more than the fellow who led that gentle-as-a-hound-dog mustang into this town."

Arky laughed, nodded, and grinned at the crowd. "Well, now, I'll tell you, you got me that time. This is quite a joke you're a playing on old Arky Blue, yes-sir-ree. But, I'll tell you what I'll do. I'll take them odds at that price. But, this gent has to ride her down in one sitting, using his saddle. He don't get no second try. Not for this money."

"Won't need one," Rattlesnake Jack said.

"Fairly and bravely spoken," Arky blustered. "Now who's going to hold the stakes?"

"I will if you're a-willing," Dil offered. "We've pooled our money for this bet and I'm known locally as a fair man."

"I can tell you are," Arky nodded as he pulled out another roll of cash and counted out sixteen hundred dollars.

Not a wrangler spoke. No one could remember ever seeing that amount of money at one time in Texas before or since the war.

"And now I'm waiting for your eight," Arky said grimly.

Dil counted the pool's resources into a neat pile on the table next to Blue's wager.

"One ride for the wager until he's throwed or she quits," Arky said loudly.

Dil nodded. "Until he's throwed or she quits."

Arky grinned and took his time studying the anxious faces that surrounded him. "Let's get to it."

A cheer rang out that rattled the windows and shook the rafters of the place as Arky led the procession through the swinging doors of the Bale-O-Cotton. Arky gathered up the mare and took his directions to the local livery corral where the spectacle could be witnessed by one and all.

No one noticed a pair of threadbare, saddle scarecrows that had just ridden into town and were meagerly watching the procession. Lord knows that if they had it might have put a damper on the whole shebang. These boys looked like two cats that had been accidentally nailed in a barrel for a week. Their ponies were so thin, knock-kneed, and rough-haired that it was a certainty the only load they could carry were the almost-as-bad starved riders on their backs. Without knowing anyone they dismounted and straddled up to the corral fence with the rest to see the goings on. They happened to position themselves right next to old Dil Townsen.

As the boys were saddling the Black Queen, Dil took a sniff of the air and decided that something musta died nearby in the last week before he realized the half-starved wretched condition of the pair standing beside him.

"You boys all right?" Dil asked as he gave them a gander.

A big-nosed, pocked-faced imbecile with a six-inch handlebar moustache answered. "Yes, sir. We could use a little work on one of the outfits if anyone's looking. We just came home from the war and need to build a stake."

Dil nodded. "I don't know about work but I'll sure as hell stand you boys to a steak dinner when this is over. You look as though you need it."

The imbecile nodded a thank you. "We been living on leftover army issue Johnny cake and shot rabbit for the last two months just trying to get back to Texas."

Dil nodded again. "Didn't see too many rabbits I take it."

"That's a fact."

"Well, who are you boys, anyway?"

The imbecile smiled and removed his hat. "Red River Sam Bonnet, thank you kindly. This is my partner, Ty Lee Driscoll."

Dil looked past Bonnet and gazed upon Driscoll. He was about the sorriest lot of raggedy-ass bones, hair, and hide a man could imagine without waking up in the middle of the night with the screaming fever fits. Dil shook his head in sad consternation. "And they allowed you boys to fight in this condition?"

"We fought them Yankees till they told us it was over and we should go home. So here we are ready to start a new life."

"We get this ride done and I'll feed you boys. That's the least I can do. Right now, we want to see old Rattlesnake Jack here ride down the Black Queen."

Driscoll mumbled softly, producing an immediate chuckle and a nod from Bonnet.

"What's that he said?" Dil asked.

"Ty Lee says that feller won't last more than four jumps. Says that mare will pile him square and sharpen her teeth on his ass before he can be rescued."

Dil was immediately concerned. "What makes you say that?"

Driscoll looked a little sick. "You don't have no money on this ride, do you?"

Dil shook his head. "Come on, hombre. What makes you say that?"

Driscoll turned back to the fence and leaned on the rail, pointing as he spoke. "He's got his saddle too far back and his stirrups too long. He's going to wedge into the saddle and try to muscle her down when he needs to use a light touch. He's too wide-shouldered and top-heavy to stay on that mare the way he's going to try to ride her. He'll try to strong-arm her and that's what she's a-wanting. She'll make three or four stiff legged jumps to jar his nuts loose, then do a wheel about on her back feet and send him a-flying. Just about the time he thinks he caught up with her, they'll be a-going in different directions."

"And you could do better?" Dil asked.

Driscoll didn't answer so Red River Sam took the reins. "Damn right he can do better. There ain't a man living that can stay a bronco or shave a steer better than this man. I've seen him make horses go into battle that were too poor to eat and then nurse them thirty more miles to the next fight with nothing more than an encouraging word and an ear rub. I've seen him ride the worst green broncos the Confederate cavalry had to offer and in less than an hour turn them over to a private, house broke and eating out of his hand. This is the best horseman that ever threw a leg over the cantle of a saddle. Even old General Forrest hisself said that Driscoll was the finest natural born cavalry rider and horse breaker in the entire Confederacy. God strike me dead if I didn't hear the words myself."

Dil went wide-eyed. "Is that a fact?"

"It is."

Dil turned to Driscoll. "Is that the truth of it?"

Driscoll looked to his feet. "I ride a little."

Dil turned to watch Rattlesnake Jack gather the reins and put his foot in the stirrup. "We'll see, by God. We'll see."

Old Jack swung into the saddle, drew up his reins, and dug those sharpened spurs hilt deep into her flanks.

"Why'd he want to do that for?" Ty Lee mumbled.

The Black Queen hunkered down as Jack set his weight into the saddle, but when them spurs found their mark, she fare-thee-well exploded into a stiff-legged, bone-jarring, detonation of full-blown, head-down, broncobusting, gut-wrenching vaults. As powerful as Rattlesnake Jack was, he could no more keep her head high than drag a ton bull with a greased lasso. She made four leaps into the middle of the corral, growling, farting, and groaning with each surge of energy. Old Jack flopped like a rag doll as he tried to find her rhythm. It looked like he was just about to catch up when she wheeled about and launched old Jack into the sky. He hit the ground headfirst and shattered like a Christmas tree ornament as those sharpened spur rowels dug into his own back.

True to form, the Black Queen wheeled about again and made for the wreck that used to be Jack. It took four men to drive her back and drag the remains of Jack to the corral fence. They shoved him through the space between the running poles and piled him neatly in some fresh horse apples on the far side. The entire affair had been a full-blown disaster.

"Har. Har. Har." Arky Blue laughed as the rest waited in silence to see if Jack would stir with life after they dug the dirt out of his mouth. "I guess that was about the worst ride I've ever seen. This was you boys' ringer? Hell's fire! My grandma coulda made a better showing."

Dil Towsen's mouth fell open as he witnessed the catastrophe. He turned to Red River, his eyes wide with wonder. "Amazing! It was just as your man said it would be."

Red River nodded grimly and looked to Driscoll for an appraisal.

"I thought he would do better than that," Ty Lee whispered.

As the men cornered the Black Queen and jerked Jack's saddle, Arky Blue swaggered over to Dil Townsen. "Well, sir, I'll tell you, I almost feel bad about taking your money. You boys ain't the wranglers I heard you was. I guess I'll need to head farther south to find a real vaquero to bring this mare to justice."

The men gulped as Dil counted out the money. Some of them had their life savings…meaning five or ten dollars…invested in that ride. But as bad as they hated losing the money, they hated Arky Blue's digs and scurvy remarks even more.

Dil watched Arky fold his wad and give the surrounding crowd one of his toothy, haughty grins. "Pretty sad, gents. I guess that was just plain heartrending. Old pretty boy there has about as much grace in the saddle as an anvil."

Dil Townsen's face looked like a freshly chiseled gravestone. As Arky turned to walk away, Dil asked, "You ain't through, er you?"

Arky held up in mid stride. "Now, that all depends. I figured you boys was cleaned out."

Dil leaned against the corral fence. "You got twenty-four hundred dollars there. You up to risking it on another ride?"

Arky eyed Townsen carefully and smiled his sick, twisted best. "You got another rider that wants to take a toss?"

Dil nodded. "I do. And I'll bet my ranch against your poke at two-to-one."

There was an audible gasp from the crowd. The H-7 was a damned fine place; too fine to risk on this deal.

Even Arky was taken aback. "Forty-eight hundred dollars? That I can't manage." He paused and thought out his finances. "I'll go fifteen hundred at two-to-one…after I see your man, that is."

Dil Townsen turned and pointed a gnarled finger at Driscoll. "There he is."

Ty Lee shifted on his feet, straightened, and removed his hat like he was being introduced to a school marm.

Arky's eyes darted quickly to Townsen to check if he was serious. "Who's he ride for?"

"Both these boys ride for the H-7," Townsen said bluntly.

Red River and Ty Lee exchanged glances but held their composure.

Arky nodded, struggling to accept the credibility of the claim. He gave the wretch closer inspection. Ty Lee was dressed in ragged, grimy Confederate gray. One of his boot toes was torn loose from its sole and the heels were so overrun that it was a wonder he could keep his balance. His filthy hat brim drooped about his ears and his black hair draped over his collar. He was scarecrow thin and he had the look of a drowned rat in a stock tank. "I don't want to offend but is this feller healthy enough to get on the mare, let alone ride her?"

Dil turned to Ty Lee and smiled. "Well, what about it? You up to riding this mare?"

Ty Lee's eyes hardened. "Yes, sir. I'd give her a go."

The crowd drew a breath in unison as it waited for Arky's reply.

Arky shook his head. "I don't want any part of a killing. This feller ain't up to it and I think we all know it."

Dil Townsen now had his turn to dig. "Must be that carpetbagger courage you were speaking of."

Arky Blue's features hardened. "The hell you say. All right, I'll put up the money against a quitclaim deed to your ranch. But, I want you to know that I don't welch and would draw a damned fine line against a welcher."

Dil nodded grimly in spite of the offensive insinuation. "Let's get a paper and write it up."

As pen and paper were gathered and the witnesses assembled round to watch the ceremony, Red River and Ty Lee waited by the corral fence.

"Well, pard," Red River said. "It looks like we got us a job offer. What do you think?"

Ty Lee shook his head. "It'll be all right. He seems straight enough."

"I hope you don't think I talked out of turn. I mean, I never intended for you to risk your neck like this."

Ty Lee leaned over the rail and studied the Black Queen. "All those days of the war. How many good friends have we had to say goodbye to? This ain't nothing no matter how it turns out."

Red River shook his head. "She could hurt ya, pard."

Ty Lee turned to get his saddle from his pony. "'Tain't nothing," he said softly.

The wranglers saddled her up and got ready to hold her head so Ty Lee could get his foot in the stirrup. He waved them away, slipped his hand close to the bit shanks and held her nose next to his face. He spoke softly to her and gently rubbed his hand under her chin, kind of like a mother comforts her fretting babe. He and that mare stood there in the middle of that corral for nigh to five minutes talking and getting to know each other. Finally, Ty Lee smiled, spoke another soft word, and eased into the saddle.

She took her four jumps and spun around. Ty Lee stayed with her. She tried it again. Ty Lee hung in a little tighter. She bucked her heart out for nigh on to twelve minutes and Ty Lee Driscoll clung to her back like he had been growed out of it. Old Ty Lee and that mare took on the appearance of a finely tuned New England glider as each part swayed in rhythm against the other. Witnesses to this day say that it was just about the prettiest thing they'd ever seen.

Suddenly, she quit. We're not talking a run out, mind you. She just plain quit and stood in the middle of that corral like a Jersey cow waiting for the milk stool and the bucket.

There was dead calm in the crowd as Ty Lee eased himself to the ground. He gave the mare a pat on the neck, jerked the saddle, and walked to the corral fence.

"Poetry. Pure poetry," Dil Townsen whispered.

Arky Blue looked like he just swallowed a plug of chew whole. He turned to walk away.

"What do you want for her?" Townsen asked.

"She's your horse," Arky Blue said. "He rode her fair and square. I'm cleaned out and she has no more value to me." He mounted up and rode away, never to be seen in Williamson County, or Texas for that matter, again.

Townsen counted out the original losses to his partners and kept the profits for himself. When it was over he turned to Red River and Ty Lee. "You boys got a job on the H-7 as long as there is such. Take the mare, Driscoll. She's yourn."

Ty Lee nodded. "Thank you, Mr. Townsen. You say she's mine to do with as I like?"

"Yes, sir. Now let's get you boys a well-deserved steak dinner."

Ty Lee opened the corral gate and gathered the Black Queen's halter rope. He led her into the open and slipped the halter. "Go on. Get!" he said.

The mare took off into the mesquite at a dead run and without a backward glance.

Sam watched it all a-grinning and said nothing.

Ty Lee looked at his partner and smiled. "Her war is over too."

Red River Sam nodded and pulled his hat close over his eyes. "Let's go eat that steak."

The Murder Steer

The cowpuncher was watching his bacon fry in his camp skillet nigh on to sundown when the youngster returned from checking the picket line. The youngster seemed unsettled as he nestled down next to his saddle on the far side of the fire.

"What's your problem?" the puncher asked. "You look like you just seen a spirit."

The kid shook his mop. "I guess maybe I did. It was the dangdest thing I ever saw. I guess my eyes were playing tricks on me."

The puncher poured coffee into the youngster's tin cup. "Go on. Amuse me. Spit it out."

The kid took the cup and set it down quickly, spilling a quarter on the ground. "Damn! That's hot! I was checking the horses like you said when I heard a movement in the brush back yonder. I gave a look-see and a big old lineback steer shook out of the mesquite. The thing is I thought I saw a crude, haired-over brand running clear along his side. I ain't for certain but I think it said MURDER." He shook his head again. "Heck, it was probably just the coming night playing tricks on my eyes. Nobody would scar up a critter like that."

The puncher held out his hand. "Give me your plate. This bacon's ready for eatin'. It was a black steer with white running along his back and belly white running a quarter up his flanks. One horn is turned slightly down and he's got some age on him."

"Can't say for certain. He was black and white but I was too busy reading his brand to notice much else."

"Son, you just got yourself a look at the Murder steer. There ain't a handful of men living that can make that claim. Some say it's a sign of good luck and a feller is blessed for seeing it. Others claim it to be a warning from the devil and you better be damned careful of your ways for a spell. Either way, you're one of a very few." He handed the plate of bacon with a ration of pintos over to the youngster.

"Thank you, kindly," the youngster said as he admired the crisp back fat and wild onions on his plate. "What the tarnation is a Murder steer?"

The puncher poured himself a fresh cup and fished a strip from his skillet. "You want the whole story or just a bit?"

The kid lounged back against his saddle. "It's early. Spin me the whole yarn."

"It was twenty years ago, back before they disbanded the Western Battalion of the Rangers. All this country hereabouts was open range with four of the big outfits sharing it. It weren't good for nothing just like today so the outfits kept outriders along the fringes to keep the cactus boomers pushed back on home range. This here country of rocky red hills and scrub mesquite was hard on cattle and cowboys to boot. The boomers would go wild and many a wrangler broke his neck or got laid up proper trying to lasso them. They called this scrub Worthless Mesa and it was a general agreement that anybody with any gumption would be too proud to claim it. Still, cattle drift and every green-up each of the outfits would send in riders to gather the winter strays and sort them out. Main camp for all the outfits was Red Box cause it was the only canyon where water springs from the rocky ledges. It was a natural tank for the linebacks to come for water and a natural box canyon was an easy spot to hold them for the sortin'. Heck, if fellers used their heads, a fair majority of them critters would catch themselves in dry times just a-coming for a drink.

The biggest outfit was the Slash Nine and as usual they sent the most men cause they would end up with the most cattle when it was all said and done. That year the Nine bunch was run by a range foreman named Blu Packett. Now, old Blu was a cocky sort of gent with an eye for the ladies and a weakness for the spotted pasteboards. He was something of a gent favoring concho chullas and nearly always sporting a black bib shirt and fancy Mexican sombrero for a sky shade. Most men thought fairly high of him if he weren't in the jug and busting a string of losing hands. When old Blu was a-drinking and gambling he could get plum spiteful and he was known to hold a grudge.

The next biggest outfit was the Arrow run by Arnold Hernandez, a half Mexican gent whose mama was a German immigrant girl who'd taken up with his daddy and was disowned by her family for her foolishness. Everybody called him Arny and his ancestors were land granted this whole end of the plateau before the rebellion, but the best Arny could do was manage a scrub outfit running a poor water range between the Nine and the Broken Bar Cross. He was a quiet sort they say, but more like a deceitful bronc that yearns to take a bite out of you when your back's turned or you're distracted from remembering his temperament. You can never tell what a Mexican is really thinking and Hernandez had just enough beaner in him to be that sort. He didn't pack no handgun but carried a six-inch, double-edged Arkansas toothpick in his belt.

The Broken Bar Cross wasn't much of an outfit and it didn't last long after this affair. Its owner, Doc Freisen, got found out with a running iron in his saddlebag and a herd of fresh brand-altered boomers a few months later. A hemp necktie ended the Cross's business dealings that next morning. But that was a few months after this story and the outfit was represented by a lunger called Four-Bit and three other hard-case, grub line riders. They were there to get the boss's share of his rightfuls and a little more if possible, but not much else. They was generally a sorry lot by most accounts.

The other outfit of note was Dil Townsen's H Bar Seven. Dil was long in the tooth by that time so he sent his two prize vaqueros, Red River Sam Bonnet and Ty Lee Driscoll and their pack of hounds, to do the judging and sorting for the outfit. He only sent two wranglers because he knew he was sending the best. Red River Sam was a colorful sport who could shake out a gut line better than most any man and he had Townsen's complete trust. Driscoll was a lame-between-the-ears scarecrow but could ride anything a man could saddle, fair wind or foul. He was the gent who rode down the Black Queen back in '66 and did the Pecos Drift in four days when the best any other rider could manage was five and a bit. Probably no better horseman ever gathered his boot in a stirrup, but Ty Lee was dumb as a post and needed some guidance to find his way to breakfast, even on a good day. Totally devoted to Driscoll were five of the nastiest, green tick bit, mean-natured, inbred hounds ever assembled in Texas. No man in camp had the courage to turn his back on any of them as he might just as well turn his back on a rabid skunk or a vengeful Comanche. The only security they had was that those curs loved fighting cattle and each other so much more that they seldom got around to going after anything else. Still, a man kept his six-gun handy if he was afoot and the pack was near.

It was Townsen's turn to supply the grub wagon. The camp cook for that round up was a Bar Seven nigger by the name of Candle Corn. I've heard many a story about Corn. He had a mighty temper and a butcher's blade to match but he was the best cook and finest camp doctor, or Psalm reader, whichever was most appropriate, to ever line out a chuck. He was famous throughout the plateau and a fine friend of many a cowhand, as long as you didn't bitch about his biscuits or steal none of his apple pie fixins. Then your life was in your own hands cause nobody crossed Candle about grub fixin' or camp running. Nobody knows for sure how many jammed fingers he lopped off, broken bones he set, stitches he took, haircuts he gave, or boils he lanced during his Dutch oven years. For all intents and purposes it was Candle Corn who ran the show concerning everything that wasn't cow bones and hide. He allowed card playing at his fire but he didn't tolerate no whisky drinking until it was time to break camp and head for home. Then he'd likely take a swig or two himself in the spirit of a farewell celebration.

The first days in camp were like most, I guess, as the boys waited on straggler outfits, dug out a latrine, repaired the catch fence, and lined out the country. Ty Lee and his hounds were driving in a passable herd before the Arrow and Cross outfits even rode in. Once they did, the whole bunch saddled up at dawn and didn't show in camp again until sundown or later for the next five days. Most of the time those boys only had a few of Candle's dodgers to cheat their bellies at noon and get by until beans and back fat that evening. When they were through scouring the mesa, they had nearly seven hundred head milling in the Box and only had to shoot two bulls, a mossback cow, and one dog for taking after them. It looked to be a right good year for everyone.

But unbeknownst to most was the fact that Blu Packett and Arny Hernandez were packing a grudge for each other. It all started over a disputed watering hole that lay near the line between the Slash Nine and the Arrow. Packett had taken it upon himself to run off some of the Arrow cows and let his herd water free. Arny considered that pond to be his and although he didn't mind a man watering his herd on a pass by, he took some offense that his own cattle were denied water for several days while Blu rested Slash Nine cattle up and they free grazed on Hernandez grass. Harsh words were spoken and the threat of gunplay sworn before the various interests parted company. Since Blu was a foreman on wages, Hernandez took his cause up with Sam Bridges, the owner. Bridges, in turn, dressed Blu down in front of his riders and told him that he wouldn't tolerate such doings again. Blu didn't quit the outfit, which was the honorable thing, but kept on with the Nine because some say he was sweet on Bridges's daughter and fancied himself the future owner of the whole shebang. He never forgave Hernandez for going over his head regarding the matter and held a grudge for being dressed down because of a Mexican. Blu was out of line on the matter but sometimes a man can't see the forest for the trees or is blinded by the flirty ways of a comely gal of property. Most say he never was in the running as far as she was concerned. He was cool around Hernandez and his mind-set was mirrored by the Mexican. Generally the pair of them just steered clear of each other and went about their business with none of the other outfits the wiser.

When it came to splitting up the herd, Red River Sam Bonnet was elected the brand judge and the ownership of calves was either decided by him or negotiated by the head man from each outfit. This normally isn't too difficult a task, as any calf sucking the teat naturally went with his mamma and it was early enough in the season that most calves were small. Any brands not associated with one of the outfits were turned over to those closest to that brand so the cattle could be drifted back on home range, but that never amounted to more than a dozen or so cattle. It was also generally the practice to brand and work the calves on the spot while the cattle were handy, so several irons were kept hot and all calves worked and separated at one time. It was a busy time and the men kept hard at it.

The one redeeming grace was that Candle Corn was rustling up some shining fine grub and the eating was plum larapin. For sorry ass outfits like the Cross, those boys had never eaten so good, so they were in no hurry to break camp and go back to the belly cheater of that spread. It quickly became evident to all that those boys were stalling just to get another day or two of three squares before lighting out. But with the apple pie and corn bread as sweet as shortcake that Candle was dishing out, nobody could get too upset at Four-Bit and his riders for taking advantage when they could, especially since the Cross had a reputation of being a hardtack and raw bean outfit.

They were getting close to the end when Four-Bit talked some of the boys into a little low stakes poker to pass the evening. Gathered round the blanket were Blu Packett, Ty Lee Driscoll, and a couple of Slash Nine wranglers. Everyone knows that it takes six to work out a solid poker game, so Four-Bit was looking for another man when Arny Hernandez happened by. After some persuasion, Arny joined in the game, "for a hand or two, but no more," he said.

Now, lo and behold, they played four hands of poker and Arny won three. Arny could see that Blu wasn't taking it too well so he begged out of a fifth. That didn't sit well with Blu either. There were some words but the others agreed that Arny had said from the get-go that he was in for only a few hands and he could rightly walk away without a grudge being held. Blu backed down but it was just one more bit of salt rubbed in a festering wound.

The next morning the outfit gathered round the tailgate for biscuits, back fat, and coffee. Arny was walking away with his vittles when Blu sort of nudged up against him and sent his grub a-flying into the dirt. Arny didn't say a word but turned back to the line for another helping.

"I guess Hernandez gets double shares this morning," Blu blustered. "But that's what I guess should be expected from a pepper."

Now, everyone there knew what was afoot and the place got as quiet as a graveyard. No one knew for certain how Arny would take the comment. Blu was hankering for a fight and it was up to Arny as to whether he'd oblige him or not. Blu had thirty pounds on him and Arny didn't carry a gun. Still, when a man is getting dogged his pride will tend to even the odds. Arny may have got whipped but a bully like Blu would usually never have the gumption to try a second time. At least that's the way most figure it.

Candle Corn took the lead. It was his fire and his right. "There's plenty," he said as he shoved a slice on a biscuit and held his paw out for Arny's cup.

That should have settled the matter but Blu was on the prod. He shook his head and leaned up against the wagon wheel as Candle filled the cup and returned it to Arny. "I shoulda guessed the likes of you'd stick together," he snarled. "Peppers and niggers. Hell, he can have mine to boot." He threw the biscuit on the tailgate and pitched his dregs into the fire as he stomped to his pony.

Ty Lee and Red River were closest to Candle. They could see the fire build in Candle's eyes and knew that his temper was a-rising.

"I wouldn't pay too much mind," Red River grinned. "Sometimes, early in the morning, a gent has to get the meanness out of his system. Old Blu never did let looking the fool interfere with his glory."

"Amen," Ty Lee nodded.

Candle gave it some thought, nodded, and went back to dealing out the biscuits. But he didn't smile and he didn't look up as the others got their feed. Old Blu was trying to pick a fight with Arny and almost got more than he bargained for his trouble. Old Candle was every bit as big as Blu and a hell of a lot meaner when it came to scrapping. Blu may have lived but he'd a-damn sure been missing body parts afore the fracas was over.

"How about another hand of poker tonight?" Red River asked as he and Ty Lee mounted their ponies.

"I don't think I'll join ya, pard," Ty Lee shrugged. "The fun's gone plum out of it."

"You can say that again. Old Blu is hell bent for trouble, that's for sure."

"Yeah, well, we got shovels in the wagon and there's plenty of clay to bury him in," Ty Lee said has he turned his pony for the herd. "Old

Arny don't look like much but I'm betting he's leather tough and snake mean when he gets riled. The quiet ones are always that way, don't you know."

"Kind of reminds me of another gent I know," Red River said with a grin. Then quieter to himself, "I think you just wrote your own epitaph, partner."

Well, that day and night passed pretty quiet. Blu was sullen and Arny kept his distance. The only worry came when Blu held out his plate for a serving of evening stew. Candle Corn stared at him and let the plate rest empty for a while.

"I wouldn't take it kindly if this grub ended up in the dirt. A fellow can get mighty hungry around here if he don't know how to manage his chow," Candle said.

Blu shook his head and looked to the ground. He was properly given notice and it sure weren't worth fighting over after a long day in the saddle. Besides, the stew smelled damn good.

Candle gave him a nod and plopped a ladle full on his plate. As far as he was concerned the affair was ended.

It was the last night before breaking camp but no yarns were spun and no poker game developed. Everyone sort of kept to himself and most turned in early.

About mid-morning they finished up sorting the dregs of the herd. Since none of them were branded and most were sorry, it was the custom to divide them up one critter to each outfit in turn. They came to a scrawny little lineback with a twisted neck and one horn hung low. Without saying anything Arny rode up and started the varmint toward his herd. Red River let it pass, it being Arny's turn and all.

Blu put his pony forward and called out. "That's a Slash Nine steer."

"How so?" Red River asked. "He ain't wearing no brand."

"I know that steer." Blu said. "He's Slash Nine."

Red River didn't see it. "Well, pick out another to take his place. Hell, it ain't carrying a brand and it ain't like he's some prize."

Blu shook his head. "No, it's Slash Nine and I mean to have him."

Arny held up and swung his pony around. It's funny how a man can let things pass then all of a sudden have his fill. Arny had had his. He waved a no and motioned to the remaining catch. "Choose another. It is my turn and the steer is mine."

"No, by God, I won't have it, Hernandez. That's a Slash Nine steer you're taking. You've had everything your way this trip but it's coming to an end now and proper."

By this time Ty Lee had rode up. "What does it matter? That damned crow bait probably won't live to make it back to home range."

"Stay out of this, Driscoll," Blu slurred. "This here's between me and the pepper."

Even old Four-Bit was disgusted. He leaned over his horn and motioned to the catch. "Hell, I'll settle it. Let him have the steer. You can have our share of the next one up. Two for one. How's that?"

"No, it's that steer I want and that steer I'll take." Blu was shaking with anger by then.

It got real quiet there in the dust, the sweat, and the flies. Everyone watched Arny to see how he'd do. It was his play.

Arny looked down at his saddle and shook his head. The muscles tightened along his jaw. "No. No more. The steer goes with me."

Blu looped his reins around his horn, stepped to the ground and slid his holster forward. "And I say no. Now what the hell are you going to do about it, Mex?"

"Have you completely lost your senses?" Red River snapped. "What the hell is wrong with you?"

Arny stepped down from his horse and pulled his blade from his belt. He wasn't wearing a gun. He let the tip of that blade balance on the long finger of his right hand, the handle balanced against his wrist. "I will tell you what is wrong with him, amigo. He has a sickness burning inside of him like many gringos I have known. It is not the steer. It is everything, isn't it? You want it all."

"Somebody give this bastard a gun!" Blu yelled. "We'll settle this right now and for good."

Arny shook his head and stepped toward him. Barely nine feet separated them. "I do not need a gun. Not for the likes of you. If you want the steer, take it, if you can."

"This is murder," Red River said. "I won't have no part in it."

It was then that Candle Corn walked up. He had been watching from the cook fire and came for a closer look. He studied the way that Arny held his blade and smiled. "Go on. If Blu wants a fight, let him have it."

Blu grinned and tensed for the draw. "That's right. And, when I'm through, you're next."

Blu hesitated. There was a madness in his eyes and his teeth gleamed like ivory in the center of his grin. "Make your play. Cause if you don't I'm gonna kill you where you stand."

Arny nodded, then quicker than a rattler he flicked his wrist underhanded and put that six-inch blade in the center of Blu's chest. Old Blu hadn't even had time to go for the draw. He just looked at the knife hilt deep in his heart and then down at his empty hand, sort of like he couldn't believe what had just happened. He rocked back and spread a cloud of dust and cow shit with his landing. Most figure he was dead before he hit the dirt.

Candle Corn calmly walked up to Blu and checked his vitals. "Deader than a skillet," he said coolly. "You were right about one thing, hoss. Old Blu never did let looking like a fool interfere with his glory."

"I guess he needs burying," Red River said as he looked over his shoulder toward the remainder of the Slash Nine crew. "And, I suppose someone ought to break the news to his outfit."

"There might be trouble," Arny said as he made a shadow over the body.

"Anybody here see anything but self-defense?" Red River asked.

"I don't know what else you'd tag it," Four-Bit said. "He'd a-killed Hernandez for sure."

Candle slipped the blade from Blu's chest and wiped the blood on his apron. "You might need this," he said as he offered it to Arny. "It might be that the crew will want to take him back to the Slash Nine. Blu may have had some kin, I'm thinking."

Arny motioned to one of his men. "Turn the steer loose. I want no part of him."

"Don't send him our way," Four-Bit said. "I'm thinking that there scrawny lineback is cursed for sure."

Ty Lee shook out his line, put a loop round the steer's horns, dallied up, and made for the branding fire.

"You ain't figuring on putting our brand on him?" Red River asked as he followed along.

"Nope," Ty Lee said. "I figure this steer is cursed and no outfit'd want anything to do with him. I'm a-gonna fix him so that never happens. Lay a loop on him so we can stretch him out."

Well, they strung him down and stretched him out right in front of the branding fire. Ty Lee gave his line to Four-Bit, stepped down from his pony and drew up the slash iron. Quick as you please, he burned MURDER across the side of that poor critter and then let him free.

Ty Lee gathered his lasso and mounted. "I figure that'll do it. Fair warning to anyone. It's their hide if they want him but they need the warning just the same."

By that time all the riders had gathered round the fire. Every man agreed that it was the proper thing to do. They buried old Blu under a mesquite and nailed his hat above the grave for a marker. They say that hat hung on that tree for several years before it rotted away. They still call that tree the blue mesquite and it's a popular gathering place for the outfits to this day. I guess old Blu was good for something after all."

The wide-eyed youngster whistled long and low. "Now that is a yarn if I ever heard one. Heck, I know where that tree is. I guess everybody hereabouts does. So, what happened to Arny? Did the law give him trouble?"

The cowpuncher shook his mop. "Nope. Back in them days there wasn't much said about such doings. Blu was dead and the matter ended there. As for Arny, he got hold of some bad water a few months later and died of the drizzlin' trots. It wasn't long before the whole affair would have been forgotten except for that old steer showing up from time to time. I wonder how long it will be afore that old steer cashes in his chips."

The youngster pitched his dregs and stared into the fire. "Could be he never will."

"Could be," the puncher said.

The Dark Man

Merciless spring winds had driven the fire through the open prairie grassland with frightening efficiency. A broad band of black, smoldering earth five miles wide and fifteen miles long left nothing unscarred in its path. As the riders made their way toward Robert Irvine's homestead, they recognized the burned corpses of coyote, rabbit, deer, and even cattle still smoldering where they fell.

"My God, Mister Print. How could anyone have survived this?" Uncle Sam Jones asked.

Print Olive shook his head and sighed. "I'm afraid it will cost Irvine his life. I've heard that his burns are terrible." He cast a determined look toward his son, Thad. "Look here now, we won't say that to the woman. Let's be mindful of her feelings when we talk to her."

"You do the talking, Dad. I wouldn't know what to say to her."

Olive nodded and urged his sorrel forward.

Nadine Irvine saw the riders coming at a distance. A black swirling ash cloud wisped along behind their ponies and drifted in the gentle wind. She stepped to the door of her soddy and brushed an errant lock of hair from her eyes to see them better and to try to present some sort of suitable appearance. She did not recognize any of the riders—a tall bearded black man in his fifties and two compact, dark-featured white men. She was anxious and gently urged her three children behind her skirts as she held her ground at the doorway.

"Hello to the house," the older white man said. "We have come to help your family."

She managed a smile as she studied his features. He was a round-faced man, dark complexion, black deep-set eyes, and a wide mouth under a heavy moustache. "I don't believe I recognize you, sir."

He held up his horse and folded his hands across the saddle horn. "I. P. Olive, ma'am. I run a herd up on the Sawlog."

She tensed. She knew his reputation. "What can I do for you?"

"We heard of your troubles. I've come to offer my help. How fares your husband?"

"He is in Dodge. The doctor tells me that his burns are serious. We are praying for him."

"He saved the cattle?"

She managed a weak smile. "Yes, he managed to drive them to out of the path of the fire. But when he tried to get back to us, his horse fell and the fire overwhelmed him. He left the cattle to the west to manage on their own. I haven't had time to see to them."

He nodded. "You are fortunate that the wind drove the fire so quickly past your soddy so there wasn't time for the roof to catch fire."

"Yes, but the children and I were very frightened. It was awful."

Olive looked down at the earth as if in thought. "Yes, ma'am. I'm sure it was." He hesitated. "I have a proposition for you. This is my son, Thad. If you are willing, he will return today with some wranglers and he will drive your cattle to my herd on the Sawlog. We will pasture them there and return them to you in the fall."

"I don't know how we would manage the rent," she said apprehensively.

"No rent. We'll manage your cattle until the fall or until such time that your husband can manage them himself. You'll have no grass for several weeks and your cattle will scatter. You'll need the income from the calves to make it through the winter."

"I don't know what to say. Your offer is quite generous."

He smiled. "Have you any food in the house?"

"We have a store in the root cellar. We'll make out."

"I'll send you a load of provisions from Dodge."

She trembled. Tears welled in her eyes. Her voice cracked. "God bless you, Mr. Olive."

He looked to the earth again, unwilling or unable to accept her blessing. "How many head do you have?"

"Fifty and a bull. At last count there were thirty-five calves but there may be more by now."

"Thad will fetch them today."

She nodded but did not speak for fear of breaking down.

He nodded. "Thad will have the supplies to you within the week."

She bit her lip and nodded again.

"We'll be on our way. My best wishes to you and your family." He wheeled his horse and started back to Dodge.

She watched them ride away and turned to her oldest daughter. "He is a most generous man. Never forget what he has done for us this day."

***

Louisa Olive watched her husband struggle to pull on his coat. She could tell that the old wounds were plaguing him. "Do you need some help with that?"

He shook his head. "I'm getting old. It's that shoulder wound from the war. It gives me more grief each year."

She thought of the ragged scar from Vicksburg on his shoulder, the four bullet scars in his chest and neck, the shotgun pellet scars on his hip from the Texas raid and wondered that he was able to manage as well as he did. He was still a powerful man and strong in spite of his accumulated wounds and years in the saddle. "Did you pack your salve?"

He pulled on his hat. "Yes, I couldn't manage without that. I shouldn't be gone more than a week. Look for me to be on the Thursday train."

"We have the church dinner Friday. I'd like you to take me."

He nodded and smiled. "I'll be back Thursday for sure. All I have to do is see that the town is ready for the herds. I'm taking Uncle Sam with me. It shouldn't take that long." He cast a look at the holstered Colt revolver and gun belt hanging on a coat peg next to the back door.

"Surely, you won't need that." She said.

"No, I gave my word. I'm through with the gun. It's just habit, that's all. Make sure that Thad gets that wagon of supplies delivered to Robert Irvine's widow. She'll need those supplies more than ever now."

"It'll be done. Thad hitched the wagon this morning and went to Zimmerman's to get those goods."

He gave her a brushing kiss, picked up his bag, and stepped out the door.

She watched him walk down the street to the corner and turn south toward the train station. She thought of the twenty-seven years of struggle and toil that they had been together. First there were the years in Texas after the war when he built the herd, the murder raid by rustlers, and the death of his brother, Jay. Then there were the years in Nebraska, the murder of his brother, Bob, and the two years Print spent in prison for lynching Bob's killers; their new start in Dodge City after the blizzard of '85, the town house, the horse ranch in Logan County, and the cattle pool on the Sawlog. They were moderately wealthy in spite of terrible losses and cruel twists of fate. He had changed after the prison sentence though—softened, carefully gauging his words and his actions. Even when the blizzard took nearly half his cattle he accepted it stoically and rebuilt his herd again. He did not rage and curse his fortune as he would have in the old days. She knew his rage wasn't gone, but he was a temperate man now compared to the old days...a better man...a good husband. She hoped he wouldn't drink too much in Trail City. Sometimes, when he drank too much the old, dark Print came back. She liked this Print much better.

***

Seven small-frame buildings and an enormous cattle loading pen next to the railroad tracks made up Trail City, Colorado, forty feet from the Kansas border. Olive owned most of the town—the saloon, the livery stable, and the dry goods store. The town had largely been his idea and he had convinced investors that the newly formed National Cattle Trail would pay off handsomely when Texas cattlemen drove their herds to the closest eastern point—the Tick Line on the Atchinson, Topeka, and Santa Fe Railroad. He hadn't counted on the new railroad reaching Fort Worth as quickly as it had, causing most of the southern herds to go there instead. But, in spite of that, one good year would allow them to break even on their investment. After that the westward driving railway would end the days of the Texas drives north to Kansas. Then, like so many times in the past, he would sell out and invest his money elsewhere.

Print and Uncle Sam stepped from the passenger car and walked the empty single street toward the saloon. The first herd was due in a week and when it arrived the place would be transformed for a few days. Lonely, bored, gaunt cowboys would fill the settlement looking for whisky, new clothes, and a good time. Print expected seven herds ranging in size from two thousand to thirty-five hundred head would arrive in quick succession. He wanted all to be ready. Twenty cases of whisky, forty barrels of beer, and four thousand dollars worth of clothing, hats, boots, gun leather, and tack waited to be consumed by the Texans. His prices would be high but with no other settlement of note within seventy miles, the cowboys would have little choice of where to spend their money. It had to be that way. He had just one season to earn his investment back. Seven herds spending five thousand a piece would do it—just seven herds. Any more would mean a profit and he knew of seven on the way for sure.

Tom Bennet stood behind the empty bar of the Trail City Saloon when Print and Uncle Sam stepped through the door. He smiled when he recognized the forty-nine year-old and his "gun nigger." He had worked for Olive off and on for nearly five years, ever since Olive first settled in Dodge City. He was glad to accept the chance to run the saloon for him. He was getting too old for cowboying. The position took him off the back of a horse and into a store—warm in the winter, dry in the rain, and plenty of whisky. "I expected you might come in on the train. What can I get you, Mr. Olive?"

Uncle Sam cut his eyes warily toward Olive when he ordered a Red Eye. Louisa had told him to watch her husband and to keep him from drinking too much, but Sam said nothing. It would do no good if he wanted a drink. Sam had been with Print through it all. He felt he knew Print Olive better than she did. She only saw one side of him. He hid his pain and his worries from her. Sam knew that inside the rough and confrontational exterior of a cattle baron there was also the weaker man—the man with wounds—deep, dark, and unsettling. Print drank to control his pain. He also drank to confront his demons. One was just as bad as the other.

Jim Kelly had been Olive's real "gun nigger." Most men considered Sam to be just a lacky—a black face to replace one nigger with another. Sam knew better. He wasn't the gun hand that Kelly had been in the old days, but Sam had stuck it out with Olive while he was in prison after Kelly left. Kelly had the bigger reputation and fame, but Sam was Olive's friend and would remain so until they shoveled the dirt in his face. So what if Print drank a little too much—he needed it to cut the pain. Sam would see that he made it to his bed all right. That's what a friend did.

Tom Bennet poured two fingers in a shot glass and turned to place the whisky bottle back on the display case behind the bar.

"Leave it," Print said abruptly. "This shoulder of mine is giving me fits and that damned laudanum makes me sick."

Tom cut his eyes to Sam for approval then said, "Sure thing." He set the bottle and absentmindedly wiped the bar with his towel.

"Do you have any help lined up when the first herd arrives?" Olive asked as he downed his glass and poured another.

"Bucky Tide is going to work the days and Al Shipman's old lady is going to help me with the night crowd."

"What about law? Have they found anyone to round up the drunks and keep the peace?"

"Starky said that old Bill Grover would act as Justice of the Peace. Old Bill worked with the Mastersons in Dodge and is hell to pay with that sawed off Greener."

Olive chuckled and poured another drink. "Old Bill will keep things in order. I'm glad they were able to get him. He's a crazy old coot, though."

"Dale Reeves hired a couple from LaJunta to run the café for him. She's a fat old heifer but damn she's a good cook. You ought to try one of her breakfasts. Her biscuits and gravy are just plain larapin."

Olive turned and gazed out the front window toward the Reeves' House Café across the narrow street. "Good. Sam and I will give her a try for dinner and breakfast in the morning." He picked up his bottle and took a seat at the table closest to the bar. The whisky was beginning to have an effect and he was mellowing. He stared at the empty shot glass and danced it softly along the table's edge. "I need to get over to the livery and see that everything is ready there."

Sam smiled. "There'll be time for that by and by."

Print looked out the window but his gaze was on the past. "This'll be the end of it. Won't be anymore trail towns after this season. The old days are gone."

Sam cut his eyes to Tom Bennet before answering. It was going to be all right. Print was mellowing rather than getting mean. "Yes, sir, Mister Print, them old days is sure enough gone."

Olive poured another glass but did not drink. He chose to study the oily texture of the dark amber liquid as he gently swirled it round the edge of the shot glass. "You remember Ellsworth? Now that was a rough trail town. Folks talk about the days in Abilene, Wichita, and Dodge but that damned Ellsworth damn near got me killed. How many years did we drive to Ellsworth?"

"Just two, Mister Print. Just two."

"That feller just couldn't believe that I wasn't cheating. Hell, he bid wild on poor hands and thought I was cheating when he lost. If it hadn't been for old Jim I'd a-been a goner that day. He shot me three times before I got a round off." He stared into the whisky. "I spent damn near six months getting over those wounds."

"Yes, sir. You was a lucky man that day. Old Jim killed him dead just in the nick of time."

Print downed his whisky. "We don't want nothing like that to happen here. Not before most of the herds are in. We don't want to be driving off business. You need to watch them games carefully, Tom. Don't let anything get out of hand."

Bennet nodded. "Old Bill will keep a tight rein on the place."

"You got to do it, Tom. Bill might not be around. If a feller is losing big, watch close. Step in and settle 'em down." Olive poured another drink. "We don't want anything like that Ellsworth business happening here in Trail City."

"I'll watch it close," Bennet said.

Print was satisfied with the answer. He squinted as he tried to recognize two cowboys going into the Reeves' House Café. "Who's them fellers over there?"

Bennet looked and shook his head. "Joe Sparrow and Ben Tate."

Olive tensed. "Joe Sparrow? What's that grub line rider doing in town?"

"Looking for work, I guess. They need some men to work the pens when the cattle come in."

Olive shook his head and downed another glass. "Can't we do better than that?"

"Most of the good men are working," Bennet said as he stepped past the bar and gazed out the window. "I don't think any solid outfit will use either one of them, but we'll need men to load out those cattle and the pickings are slim."

Olive looked back to his bottle. "I guess so. Watch that bastard. He's no good. Don't lend him any money no matter what his story. He still owes me twelve dollars." He poured another glass. "I need to get over to the livery."

"You want I should go for you?" Uncle Sam asked.

Olive shook his head. "No, I got to do it myself. We're driving several good mounts down from Logan County as replacement stock for them cowboys. I need to talk to Travers myself. We probably need to get something to eat. I need to clear my head a bit."

"You want to eat now?" Sam asked.

Print hesitated. "No, let's wait until Sparrow leaves before we go over there. I don't want to try to keep my dinner down and listen to that worthless bastard run his mouth." He poured another drink. "Besides, I promised Louisa that I'd steer clear of trouble."

Sam smiled as he recognized the irony. There was a time when Print Olive would have gone straight over to the café and demanded his twelve dollars at the point of a gun. A promise to Louisa would have meant nothing then. "*Times sure do change*," he thought. He thought it but he didn't say it.

"Looks like he's coming over here," Bennet said as he recognized Sparrow and Tate leaving the café and walking toward the saloon.

Olive shook his head and poured another drink in silence.

Sparrow bolted through the door with Tate immediately behind. He was a tall, fair-haired, thin man in his thirties. "Goddamned cheapskates. Seventy cents a day to work our asses off loading them cattle. I got me half a mind to ride out." He held up when he recognized Olive. "Well, I'll be damned. How are you doing, I. P.?"

Olive was friendly but reserved. "I'm all right, Joe. How are you?"

Sparrow blustered and made for the bar, talking as he went. "Them goddamned cheapskates only want to pay me seventy cents a day to load cattle. Goddamned cheapskates!" He thumped the bar impatiently for a glass.

"Seems like seventy cents a day ain't bad money," Tom Bennet said as he brought the whisky. "Hell, it beats cowboy wages."

"Then why the hell don't you do it and I'll run this bar and tell fellows how to conduct their business?"

Sam anxiously cut his eyes to Olive. He relaxed when he saw Print smile wryly, shake his head, and pour another drink.

"I was only saying that seventy cents a day ain't bad money for loading cattle," Tom apologized.

"Well, you keep your goddamned opinions to yourself," Sparrow snapped as Bennet poured their drinks. "I don't need to take any shit off'n the likes of you."

Bennet poured the drinks and accepted the money.

"Sons a-bitches around here. I got me a good mind just to ride out," Sparrow muttered as he downed his whisky.

"You owe me twelve dollars," Olive said softly.

"What? What's that you said?" Sparrow asked.

Print turned in his chair. His black eyes whisky-glistened. "You owe me twelve dollars."

"So what if I do? I'll pay you."

"I wouldn't think that a debtor like you could afford to be so particular about his work. And you ain't a patch on Tom Bennet's ass, so you watch your mouth."

Sparrow's posture weakened. "I know I owe you, I. P. I don't know what that has to do with this."

Print's frame trembled as he struggled to control his anger. "You come into my business a-bitching about having to do an honest day's work for a day's wages—wages that most men would be proud to take— and how you think you ought to just ride out, and owing me twelve dollars and talking to my man like that. Jesus damn! You are one worthless son-of-a-bitch!"

Sam wanted to go to Print and settle him down, but he didn't. When he was drinking there was no point in trying to intervene until after he had said his piece. It would only make him angrier.

Sparrow's eyes cut to Print's right hand to see if he had a gun in it. He spoke quietly, almost apologetically. "I guess I have a right to an opinion."

Print remained in his chair. The anger was subsiding but his eyes remained black. "Not in here you don't. You'll show some respect by God, or get the hell out."

Sparrow nodded. "I don't want no trouble, I. P. I was just a-thinking out loud."

Print looked at his glass and reached for his bottle. "That's the trouble with you, Joe. You don't think much at all. You just run your mouth."

Sparrow turned to the bar and downed his whisky. He stood quietly and allowed his anger to grow. "It's easy for you to talk down to me, ain't it? Especially, since you got your gun nigger watching my back."

Bennet stiffened and stepped away from Sparrow. Tate stepped back in the other direction. Sam's eyes cut to Print fearfully before he remembered that he wasn't armed.

Print sat stiffly. His features hardened as he digested what Sparrow had said. "You think I need anyone's help to take down a dreg like you?"

Sparrow knew he had gone too far. He held his tongue and shook his head.

"Maybe we ought to be getting something to eat, Mister Print," Sam said.

Print did not answer. His cold black stare bore through Sparrow's back.

"We used to be good friends, I. P.," Sparrow finally said. "Hell, I used to ride for you. I don't want no trouble."

Print seemed to relax. He cut his eyes to Sam. "Maybe we had ought to get something to eat."

Sam nodded and started for the door.

Print stood and glared at Sparrow's back. "The next time I see you, you better have that twelve dollars. If not, it will be the last time."

Sparrow nodded and looked down at the bar.

Sam waited and followed Print out the door.

They ordered their meal and ate in silence. Print was absorbed in his thoughts.

Sam was sipping his after-dinner coffee when Print sighed. "I guess I got carried away in there."

Sam looked up and nodded. "Well, Mister Print, Joe Sparrow ain't much of a man."

"You'd think I'd learn. Getting on the off side over a dreg like Sparrow isn't worth my worry. Hell, I'll never see that twelve dollars and I know it."

"I wouldn't worry about it too much," Sam said. "I doubt you'll ever see him again. If you do, he'll damn sure keep his place."

"It ain't the twelve dollars, anyway. I just can't abide a man that won't earn his keep and expects everyone else to pay his dues."

Sam studied him. Print was sobering and the meanness was leaving. "Yes, sir, I suppose you're right."

"Damn foolish for a man to make a threat like that when he isn't heeled."

"He wouldn't have done nothing, Mister Print. I was watching him."

"That's my point. You shouldn't have to watch a man for me. If I ain't gonna go armed, I shouldn't talk like a man who is. That don't make me much better than Joe Sparrow."

Sam set his cup on the table with a clank. "There's a big difference between you and Joe Sparrow. You don't need to run yourself down like that."

Print smiled weakly. "Thank you for that. I think we'll just head home in the morning. This damned place can run itself. I need to go home and be with Louisa."

Sam nodded. "I know she'd like that."

Print smiled. "She'd have me for breakfast if she knew about this Sparrow deal."

Sam grinned and nodded. "Yes, sir, I think she would for a fact."

They were up early and met with John Travers when he opened the livery. Print was in especially good spirits. He laughed and joked with Travers and complimented him on the appearance of the livery and the corrals.

As they left he handed Sam a five dollar gold piece. "Go down and buy our tickets. I've got some business at the dry goods, then I'll say goodbye to Tom. We'll have breakfast before heading back to Dodge."

Sam nodded and started for the train station.

"And, Sam!" Print called.

Sam turned to see Olive smiling broadly.

"Thank you for last night. Louisa would have been as proud of you as she would have been put out with me."

Sam grinned. "Yes, sir. Thank you." He turned for the station.

Joe Sparrow watched them from the window of the Trail City Saloon. He had been up all night drinking. "There's Olive. He'll probably come over here next."

Tate was trying to sleep it off in a table chair and growled an incoherent response.

Tom Bennet poured coffee into two cups and set them on the bar. "You better get out of here, Joe. I'm sure you don't want to run into Print Olive this morning."

"How many men has he killed?" Sparrow asked as he watched Print go into the general store.

Bennet shook his head. "Don't know for sure. Some say fifteen. I've heard counts as high as twenty."

Sparrow nodded. "And he wants to make me number twenty-one."

"Drink your coffee, Joe, and get out of here. Chances are that Print has forgotten all about it now that he's sober."

"Threaten my life, will he? Just who the hell does he think he is?" Joe gave a cup to Tate and sipped his own. "What's he think he's gonna do? Lynch me like Mitchell and Ketchum in Nebraska? Hell, burn my corpse so's not even my family can recognize me?"

"I'd be careful about that kind of talk," Bennet said. "Olive won't stand for it. He did his time for that. Those bastards murdered his brother. You will end up in a hole in the ground for sure."

Tate finished the coffee then set his cup on the table. "Olive's coming across the street now. We better go out the back door, Joe."

Joe shook his head. "Where you going? You lost your nerve?"

Tate nodded. "Damned straight. I don't want nothing to do with no showdown with Print Olive."

"Come on, Joe," Bennet said. "We don't want no trouble this morning."

Print stepped through the door and smiled when he saw Joe. "I was wanting to talk to you."

"The hell you say!" Sparrow yelled as he drew his revolver and fired three times.

Print clutched his chest, stumbled back to the doorway, and slid to the floor.

"Oh, my God," Tom Bennet yelled. "What have you done?"

Joe Sparrow walked calmly across the room and looked down at Olive.

Print sat upright against the doorway. He looked up at Sparrow. "Oh, Joe, don't murder me."

Joe looked down without emotion, cocked his revolver, aimed carefully, and put a round into Print's forehead.

Tate ran past his partner and through the door. "Come on. Let's get the hell out of here."

Sparrow nodded and followed Tate to their horses. They mounted and rode out of town.

***

Sam and Tom Bennet waited by the boxcar as men loaded the crude coffin containing Print's body for the trip back to Dodge City.

"There'd be several of us from Trail City at the funeral but that herd is due in any day," Bennet said. "Tell Mrs. Olive that, would you?"

"Sure, Tom, I'll tell her that. I know she'll understand."

"I suppose she'll want to sell out of this Trail City deal."

Sam shook his head. "I can't say what she'll want to do. I'm sure she'll say."

Bennet watched them slide the coffin into the boxcar. "I sure wish Print had been armed. Sparrow would have never took that last shot if he had."

Sam nodded, uncomfortable with the image.

"You know Sparrow will claim self-defense what with that threat Print made and all. And with Print's reputation, he just might get off."

Sam stepped up into the boxcar and sighed. "I know. That fellow shot Mister Print for what he used to be. Not for what he is."

"How was he supposed to know that?" Bennet asked as he handed Sam his bag.

Sam turned his eyes for one last look at Trail City. "I don't rightly know. I guess maybe he wouldn't."

The crew slid the door partially closed, the train jerked to a start, and Bennet waved goodbye.

For quite a while Sam sat by the coffin and watched the countryside as it drifted by. As the train neared the Aubrey Cut-Off, he put his hand on the top of Print's coffin and gently gave it a pat. He shook his head and said softly, "Twelve dollars."

As the train rolled on toward Dodge City, Sam sat by the coffin and wept.

Showdown Along the Cimarron

I

John McKnight stepped to the top of a sandy ridge and gazed upon the valley of the Cimarron River. He paused to catch a breath, placed the butt of his flintlock long rifle on the ground between his feet, tipped his low-crowned black felt hat to the back of his head, and enjoyed a gentle south breeze against his matted, sweat-soaked brown hair.

Tom James groaned as he led two packhorses to the crest of the dune. He scanned the broad, lush floodplain and with a sweeping gesture of his right arm, silently announced a successful crossing.

Jeemy Wilson, the next to top the crest with his packhorses, shouted a war whoop of satisfaction as he stared upon the shallow sluggish waters of the Cimarron. The graybeard had correctly predicted a two-day passage across the plain between the Arkansas and Salt Rivers.

"Looks good, don't it?" McKnight asked in his customarily quiet manner.

James grinned as he placed the butt of his rifle into the dirt and assumed a twin pose to his partner. "Couldn't look better."

Jeemy Wilson squinted and pointed a gnarled finger toward far white bluffs across the valley. "I'll bet ya them's buffalo over there to the northwest."

The rest of the brigade members topped the dune leading their pack animals toward the bottoms. John James was Tom's younger brother. David Kirkee was a bit older, in his thirties, and the smallest of the men. Bill Shearer, Alex Howard, Ben Potter, and John Ivy were men in their twenties. Frederick Howard was older and had a family in Missouri.

John McKnight was the managing partner of a profitable St. Louis trading company known as McKnight & Brady. He had received word a year earlier that his brother, Robert, was alive in a prison near Santa Fe. Ten years earlier, Robert led a trading expedition to Santa Fe, but the party vanished. John intended to find his brother, buy his freedom, and return home. Tom James and Fred Howard were old friends who needed a chance to make up for failed trading ventures along the Mississippi. If all went well, the brigade would reap a fortune from the twelve thousand dollars worth of goods purchased in St. Louis by James and McKnight.

The last man over the ridge was the interpreter, a Spaniard named Francois Maesaw. He was looked upon with suspicion and avoided by all except McKnight and Jeemy Wilson. When he wasn't advising McKnight, Maesaw kept to himself.

Approaching his seventieth year, Jeemy Wilson was of that breed of men known as "borderers." Of Scotch decent and over six feet tall, he chose to live on the frontier as civilization pushed him west. His shoulder-length white hair and chest-length beard surrounded sharp features and crystal blue eyes. A stern glare from Wilson reminded lesser men of the visage of God in his wrath. He laughed and joked with the younger men, advised the older, and treated the Spaniard as an equal. He carried a sawed-off fusel loaded with tear shot rather than a common long rifle favored by the others. A short-handled, single-bladed ax seemed to live in his right hand. When McKnight's keelboat could advance no farther up the shallow Arkansas, Wilson suggested burying the heavy goods and going overland using Osage ponies as packhorses.

"If them are buffs, we could stand to jerk a little meat," Tom James said. "We should make camp and lay in some supplies before going any farther."

"Ought to have our backs against a wall or at the top of the ridge," Wilson said. "I'd like a place where we can fort up, if need be."

As the trio led the way, the others followed as soon as they had their fill of the brackish river water. The valley was littered with buffalo manure and laced with narrow trails. Salt deposits were so thick that the men could knock off pure chunks with their knives. The herd was skittish and maintained a distance from the brigade.

Wilson reasoned that Indians were hunting the beasts. He advised the men to take a few, jerk the meat, and move on as soon as possible. By nightfall they had skinned two calves, enjoyed fresh roasts, sweetbreads, kidneys, and liver, and rested comfortably along the shore of the Cimarron.

Shortly after dawn, Ben Potter shook McKnight awake. Potter's urgency caused Tom James to jump from his own bedroll.

"Comanches are after the horses," Potter whispered hoarsely.

"How many?" James asked as he peered across the horizon toward the pony graze.

"Hell, I bet there's a hundred or more," Wilson said as he joined the others.

In the distance, a large band of riders could be seen hazing the livestock. Most were dressed only in breechcloths and leggings.

James primed the pan of his rifle. "If they get those horses, we're done for."

"They may be willing to talk if we can get their attention," Wilson said. James considered the suggestion, nodded, and ran for his goods. He drew forth a new artillery sword and buckled the scabbard about his waist. He dug out a United States flag and waved the banner from the barrel of his rifle. The Indians broke off from the ponies and approached at full gallop.

As the braves approached, McKnight spoke calmly. "Put your pieces in order, but keep the muzzles down. We want no fight, if we can avoid it. Tom, you palaver and Maesaw can interpret into Spanish if need be."

The Spaniard stepped to James's side as the warriors approached. The pair advanced to the front of the group, hands held palms forward to signify peace. The Comanche braves encircled the brigade without dismounting.

One of the leaders was of slim build with a ruined left eye. The other, a heavy shouldered man with a broad mouth, carried a newly decorated Mexican smoothbore musketoon. Neither of the men spoke immediately. Each gave the small group of whites a serious visual inspection before any attempt at communication. Finally, with sharp movements, the smaller man gave a set of signs.

James turned toward Maesaw and waited for his translation. The Spaniard watched carefully and nodded a reply.

"What does he want?" James asked.

"Gifts," Maesaw answered in accented English. "He wants gifts for crossing their hunting lands and taking their buffalo."

"How much?" James asked.

Maesaw smiled grimly. "All he can get."

"How much do you think?" James asked as he turned toward McKnight.

McKnight studied the strength of the force. There at least a hundred riders armed with Mexican flint fusels, spears, and bows. "I think we should be generous, Tom. I doubt this is a time for bargaining."

"Ask them to step down from their ponies and we'll work something out," James told Maesaw.

"I doubt they will do that. These men live on the backs of their horses. They will not step down from their mounts except for a friend," Maesaw said.

James turned toward Wilson and Howard. "Get into the packs. Give them mirrors, ammunition, knives, and the cheap calico."

As the men gathered the offerings, the one-eyed chief talked angrily with the other.

"What's his problem?" McKnight asked.

"He says we are spies for the Osage. He wants to put us under now and take the goods," Maesaw answered grimly.

"Tell him we're not. Tell him we bought the ponies from the Osage," James said.

"I think we should wait, señor. The other chief, the one called Big Star, is telling One-eye that it would not be good to kill us. He is saying that we are willing to pay and they should honor our offerings."

"I like that feller already," Wilson said quietly.

The chiefs bantered back and forth for several minutes as the men assembled their offerings. The more they debated, the more goods James ordered from the packs.

The men assembled three thousand dollars worth of merchandise: balls, powder, mirrors, knives, hatchets, bolts of cloth, and pots and pans. A line of goods was assembled between the chiefs and the traders. Finally, Big Star waved off the other and nodded. One-eye cursed bitterly and led a faction of warriors away. Once One-eye was out of sight, Big Star slipped from his pony and advanced toward James. The big Indian nodded and spoke in a friendly fashion.

"He says that we pay him great honor. He asks us to accompany him to his village and be his guest," Maesaw said.

"What do you think?" James asked McKnight.

McKnight smiled feebly and nodded. "I don't see that we have much choice. I certainly don't want to insult this character."

Wilson spat. "I wouldn't trust him, Captain. These Comanches are a funny lot."

"What do you suggest we tell him?" James asked.

"Tell him you've got to go. Tell him you got the pox. Tell him you love him so damned much you'll give him the whole kit and caboodle. Hell, tell him anything and let's get the hell out of here," Wilson answered.

"It's a long walk back to Arkansas," Frederick Howard sighed.

"A long walk, or a slow roast," Jeemy said harshly.

"If we tried to leave now, I doubt we would get far," Maesaw said. "Even if this one allows us to pass, I doubt the other would let us go far."

"I ain't going to give it all up now," Tom James said. "Maybe we can do some trading. We've got too much invested to simply walk away."

McKnight nodded. "We ain't got any choice. If I thought we could walk away from this and get out with our hair, I'd do it. It appears to me that our only option is to go with these fellows and try some trading. If we insult him now, we don't stand a chance."

The brigade members nodded and voiced support. All Jeemy Wilson could manage was a disgusted spit into the earth and a soft curse.

II

The traders and their escort entered the camp amid howls of derision, noisy conversation, barking dogs, and bawling children. Throngs of Comanche men, women, and children gathered at the edge of a substantial village meandering through the small creek-fed valley northwest of the Cimarron floodplain. Shallow canyon walls and a spring-fed stream provided protection from the elements. A low, flat-topped hill dominated the center of the site.

Big Star proudly displayed the artillery sword above his head as he led the parade through the village toward a large tipi, situated near the mound. An elderly chief wrapped in a white bear skin stepped from the tipi, mounted a pony, and haughtily waited to accept his guests.

McKnight, James, and Maesaw stepped to the front and gazed up at the imposing figure of the chief. He moved slowly and spoke with grand gestures.

After Big Star spoke to the chief, Maesaw translated the introduction. "This is Bear Shield. He is the main chief of the village. Big Star has presented you as honored guests and…" The Spaniard paused soberly.

"And what?" McKnight asked.

The Spaniard faced the partners glumly, reluctant to complete the translation. "And, says that you have brought many gifts to honor him."

"Hell's election," Wilson cursed from a few feet behind.

James cut his eyes toward McKnight. "Before they're through, we'll be lucky to leave with the shirts on our backs."

"It's the hair on my head that worries me," Wilson said.

McKnight smiled in cynical frustration. "I wonder how many chiefs we're going to have to pay off to get out of this mess?"

"Damn, John, they're robbing us blind," James said.

"We were willing to walk away from the whole thing a few miles back. If we don't pay up, we're in a worse mess than we were before," McKnight said.

James shook his head before turning toward Howard. "Bring up your ponies, Frederick. Break out the goods for our honored host."

Howard nodded and led his packhorses to James's position. James unwrapped the lashings roughly and emptied the contents for Bear Shield's examination.

"There goes another thousand dollars' worth," James said as he stepped to McKnight's side.

Bear Shield examined the trade goods and cheap bolts of cloth. He spoke quietly to Big Star and addressed Maesaw in equally reserved fashion.

Maesaw nodded and turned a tortured expression toward McKnight and James. "Bear Shield says that his people will welcome the gifts warmly. He feels that the chief of the Kamanashe should be entitled to a special gift, as was Big Star."

Tom James's face took on the appearance of a red-hot boiler about to explode. McKnight stepped in front of his partner and turned his back toward the chiefs. James relaxed as McKnight's shadow crossed his form.

"How about the velvet?" McKnight asked.

James grimaced and bit his lip. "Sure, why the hell not?"

"Why don't you go back and get it? I'll try to get Maesaw to reason with them," McKnight said.

Maesaw was uneasy. His attention drifted nervously between the anxious brigade commander and the sullen chief.

"You know, Maesaw, we don't have much left. Can't we try something else?" McKnight asked in as reserved and pleasant a manner as he could muster.

"Señor McKnight, we are at their mercy. I fear that if we refuse them, we will be dead men within the hour."

McKnight listened stoically. He knew Maesaw was no coward and his answer was not the result of cowardly logic. He turned to Jeemy Wilson.

"Well, what do you think, old timer? You've dealt with these Indians before," McKnight asked.

The buckskinner set his eyes toward the ground. "If they was Kiowas or Arapahos, you might try getting tough and bluffing your way through. But, these Comanches are a strange lot. I fear you'll end up giving them the whole shebang and they'll still show fight."

Tom James presented a roll of a hundred and seventy yards of red velvet cloth. Bear Shield felt the bolt reverently with the tips of his fingers. The master politician smiled and swelled with flamboyant generosity. He spoke boldly so the whole of the community could hear.

A warrior rode his pony to the bolt and lifted it from James's arms. He took hold of the cut end of the cloth and tossed the bolt into the air, riding away at a gallop. In seconds the red velvet was being unrolled as the populace eagerly descended upon it.

James watched in horror as his precious trade cloth was ripped and torn into blankets, robes, and fragments. "We paid six dollars a yard for that velvet."

McKnight nodded. "Maybe that will satisfy them, Tom."

Bear Shield turned toward Big Star and issued some orders before swinging his pony away from the men toward his tipi. Big Star slipped from his pony and approached McKnight and James through the throng of clamoring Indians. He spoke to Maesaw and pointed toward an open area between the mound and cliffs to the west.

"We are to make camp there for the night. Bear Shield is satisfied," Maesaw said.

"They ain't going to let us go?" Jeemy Wilson asked.

"No, we are to remain here," Maesaw answered.

McKnight nodded and motioned his group toward the mound without comment.

The men made camp without interference. They were allowed to come and go to the stream at will and prepare their evening meal in peace. As the men gathered around evening campfire there was little conversation.

Jeemy Wilson watched the sentries on the cliff tops as he sipped some coffee. "We could try slipping out when the camp's asleep, but I fear those guards will sound the alert as soon as we stir."

McKnight nodded. "How would we outrun them on foot? They'd overtake us within hours even if we were able to slip away."

"At least we could make a stand on open ground," John James said. "We're trapped like rats against this wall."

"Maesaw, how far is it to a settlement?" Tom James asked.

The Spaniard shook his head. "It is at least a hundred leagues to Nacatoche. It would take three days hard march to get there."

"No ranches or haciendas nearabouts?" James asked.

"None that I know of. Nacatoche is the closest settlement. It is in the forest. The Comanche will not go into the trees except to trade, and even then they will only come reluctantly."

"Maybe we could make the trees and they'd back off," Frederick Howard said.

The Spaniard cut his eyes slowly toward Howard and spoke solemnly. "We would not make the trees, Señor Howard."

McKnight watched his men carefully, trying to decide the best strategy. He felt that such a bold move might be necessary but could plainly see that Maesaw feared the tactic. At that moment he trusted the Spaniard's judgment more than the others did. "It might be that we have won them over. I'd hate to think we'd forced a fight that wasn't necessary. I suggest we wait to see what they do in the morning."

There was a moment of silence. His words seemed logical and reasonable. None of the men were eager for a fight that would end with their massacre.

"If worse comes to worse, I don't want us to go under like a pack of whimpering dogs. I say we make our lives as dear as possible. Make them pay a price," Wilson said.

The men voiced support.

McKnight nodded. "I agree, Jeemy. But I reiterate, we have other avenues that should be attempted before that."

"Let us firmly resolve and pledge to one another. If the worse comes, we will stand and fight like men, together and to the end," Tom James said.

Agreement spread through the brigade. McKnight did not say more. The pledge was a good idea. Men with such a mindset were easier to lead and persuade. Facing death with defiant resolve was a much easier dose of medicine to swallow.

McKnight threw the dregs of his coffee into the fire and watched the liquid sizzle and bubble on the burning embers. It seemed a good symbol of their situation.

III

Morning dawned bright, still, and hot. Dust surrounded the brigade members as they prepared their packs. Comanche activity was slow developing. McKnight observed morning activities not significantly different from St. Louis: women choring, children playing, and men going about their business.

Big Star and another Indian came to their camp on foot, dressed in formal attire, carrying a smoking pipe. The brigade members joined him at the campfire to pass the pipe. James offered tobacco and the Indian graciously accepted.

"I thank my white brothers. You have been generous and brave in your dealings. I want you to know that I will do all I can to see you safely on your way. I brought you to the camp because One-eye was waiting to rub you out," Big Star explained through his interpreter.

"May we go, then?" Tom James asked.

"No, I fear not. There will be a council to decide your fate. I will speak for you."

"Is there anything we can do?" McKnight asked.

"Perhaps more gifts. Something for Bear Shield. His voice will be the greatest."

McKnight turned to Tom James. "What about a pistol? I've got those duelers in the case."

"Maybe one," Tom James answered. "I'd save the other to put a bullet in the old bastard's heart."

McKnight nodded. Frederick Howard went to a pack and drew out a cherry wood case. He fetched one of the .45 caliber flintlocks from the box and handed the prize to McKnight.

"Give this to Bear Shield. Tell him it is a great prize and was intended as a bribe for the Spaniards in Santa Fe."

Big Star accepted the pistol. "This will do nicely. Bear Shield has no such weapon. None other in the village has anything like it."

The chiefs departed, leaving the brigade members in silence.

"That may just turn the trick," McKnight said.

"I paid a hundred dollars for those pistols in St. Louis," James said.

McKnight nodded. "Load the other and give it to me. I'll save it for later."

One-eye and his braves rode into camp from the north slope of the valley at a full gallop. The war chief guided his pony to the edge of the brigade's campsite and glared down upon the men, especially Tom James.

James returned the hot glare with a nod. One-eye mumbled a soft curse and kneed the pony towards Bear Shield's tipi.

Wilson stepped to James's side. "I wish that fellow had been a little slower showing up. I doubt he'll speak kindly in our favor."

James's expression went cold and dark. "I'll tell you one thing—I'll see him in hell if he starts a fight."

Wilson rocked his ax in his hand. "You and me both, Johnny."

Within the hour, Big Star and the other chief returned. He seemed disturbed and frustrated. "There is a problem. One-eye wants the sword."

James became indignant. "I gave the sword to you. Tell him I'll give him something else."

"No, he will have the sword or your lives," Big Star reluctantly answered.

"Piss on him. I won't give him another damn thing," James said.

"You have no other sword?" Big Star asked.

"No, that is the only one I had," James answered.

The Indian nodded and handed the blade to James. "Take it and give it to One-eye."

James took the sword. The Indian smiled as Maesaw translated James's words. "I'll make this up to you, Big Star."

"Give the sword to Black Pony to take to One-eye. I cannot give the sword for you. It would not look good."

James nodded and handed the sword to the other chief.

Within the hour several chiefs and elderly men gathered at the top of the mound. Younger men and boys started to climb the hill as well, but the older ones drove them back. Soon it was evident that a major council was being held on the hilltop.

"I don't like the looks of that," Wilson said as the brigade members watched the progress of the meeting.

The younger men and boys were gathering horses and preparing weapons. Most disturbing was that Big Star and Black Pony were not a part of the council.

"I think we should pile our goods and form a barricade around them with saddles and harness," McKnight said.

"Then it's a fight, is it?" James asked.

"I think we should close ranks and be ready to defend ourselves, if it comes to that," McKnight answered.

The group worked quietly, piling the goods in the center, surrounded by empty packs, harness, and pack saddles. As they were completing the chore, the council broke up. The old men and chiefs ambled down the slope and went to their tipis. Village activity increased as individuals gathered possessions and assembled families.

"It looks to me like they're getting ready for a move," James said.

"Maybe they're just going to leave us here and be on their way?" Wilson said.

"What do you think, Francois?" McKnight asked.

The Spaniard shook his head slowly.

Big Star returned to the barricade and cast his eyes to the ground as he spoke. "I will remember you. I will speak of you with honor."

"What's that supposed to mean?" Frederick Howard asked nervously.

Wilson shook his head and picked up his fusel. "It means we're going on a journey and he wants to bid us farewell."

Howard's expression was fearful as he turned to McKnight.

"They mean to rub us out," McKnight said impassively.

"Perhaps more gifts," Howard suggested half-heartedly.

"What for?" Tom James asked. "They'll get it all, anyhow."

"Maybe we should take these two as hostages?" Wilson suggested.

James waved the chiefs away. "No, they'd only kill them as well. They did their best. Let them go in peace."

As the lodges came down, the Indians began slowly gathering around the brigade. McKnight formed his men, shoulder to shoulder in a tight circle, facing out from the goods in the center, tomahawks and knives in their belts. McKnight stood between Tom James and Wilson. John James stood beside his brother.

The Indians constricted the encirclement, mounted men to the front, women to the back.

Tom James noticed McKnight's pale lips trembling. Maesaw could be heard mumbling a rosary prayer from the other side of the goods.

James turned to his younger brother. "I'm sorry I got you into this, John. I wish I could have given you better service."

John nodded slowly and spoke without looking at his brother. "You've got nothing to apologize for, Tom. You're a good brother and a fine man."

Tom James turned back to face the Indians. He nodded and fought back tears. "Thank you, John."

The men faced their grim foes stiffly. Only the nervous prancing of ponies broke the silence. Heat and dust enveloped the barricade.

Bear Shield forced his pony through the throng. He was dressed in the white bear robe and carried an elaborately decorated spear. The old chief glared menacingly down at the brigade. In short course, One-eye forced his pony to the chief's side. Bear Shield jammed the point of his spear toward Tom James's breast, as if calculating the distance to his heart. He placed the spear across the front withers of the animal and drew the dueling pistol from his belt. He opened the frizzen and examined the powder. Not liking the appearance, he replaced it with a fresh load. After closing the frizzen, he stopped as James's rifle muzzle slowly swept in his direction.

One-eye watched the event carefully, his eye dancing from side to side.

Finally, McKnight spoke. "I can't stand this much longer, Tom. I know he means to kill you first. I'll revenge you the instant he fires."

"Let's be done with it. I'll cleave a path through them as soon as the word is given," Wilson said.

Tom James blinked and swallowed hard before speaking. "Wait a minute. Let's not rush into this. Those two know they're dead men just as soon as we are. Let them fire the first shot."

McKnight bit his lip and nodded slowly.

Several moments passed as the Indians glared silently at the determined brigade. The smell of sweat, unwashed bodies, and nervous beasts permeated the air.

Suddenly, David Kirkee threw down his weapon, raised his hands, and stepped away from the circle.

Ben Potter whispered harshly. "What the hell are you doing?"

"I've had enough, boys. I'm going to walk out of here and let them have the damned stuff," Kirkee said.

"That cuts it," James said. "Get ready, men."

As Kirkee stepped to the encirclement of Comanches, they allowed him to pass.

"Can it be that simple?" Tom James asked.

McKnight's voice was firm. "I doubt that David gets far."

A commotion could be heard toward the outskirts of the village.

"They must have got David," McKnight said.

"The bastards," Wilson said. "Let's get this over with!"

Maesaw's voice rang out, "No. Wait, señors. They are Mexicans."

The Comanches divided as a handsome Spaniard in expensive dress forced his mount past the chiefs.

"Thank God I am in time," the Spaniard said. "I truly feared that you would be dead."

The Spaniard turned toward One-eye and spoke sternly. The chief accepted the orders without resistance. He swung his pony about and issued orders for the people to withdraw. Old Bear Shield cut his eyes menacingly toward James and without comment wheeled his horse away.

"These Comanches are our allies," the Spaniard said. "They had been told to kill any Yankees that passed through these lands. They had no way of knowing that the Spanish are no longer in control. A free Mexico welcomes you openly."

"I'm John McKnight. To whom do I have the honor?"

"Don José de Philimon, Alcalde of Nacatoche, at your service, señor."

The men gathered around Philimon. Within a few moments, David Kirkee returned and paused apart from the group. Jeemy Wilson roughly slapped him on the back.

"Don't feel so bad there, David," Wilson laughed. "For several moments, I was wishing that I had tried the same thing."

"We should go to Nacatoche immediately. I am not sure how long this truce will last," Philimon said.

"How did you know about us?" James asked.

"Big Star sent word by rider yesterday," Don José answered.

"Give me that pistol, John," Tom James said.

McKnight drew the flintlock from his belt and handed it to his partner. James walked alone toward Big Star who was gathering his wives and possessions.

Big Star turned toward James and smiled with uncertainty.

Tom James looked intently into the warrior's eyes as he spoke. "I know you can't understand a word that I'm saying, but I want you to know that I'll never forget what you did for us."

Big Star accepted the gun without examining it and spoke to one of his wives. The woman retrieved an ornamental smoking pipe.

"*Na net shay, he mi toscha,*" he said softly as he handed it to James.

Big Star mounted his pony and ordered his family to move out. He did not look back as he rode away.

James walked silently back to Maesaw and asked, "What does, *Na net shay, he mi toscha,* mean?"

Francois Maesaw paused and thought before shaking his head and answering, "He said, 'All men travel a common road.' It is meaningless."

James turned to look back toward the last vestiges of the village as Wilson stepped near.

"I wonder what he meant?" James asked as he fondled the pipe.

"Does it matter?" Wilson asked.

Tom James smiled. "No, I guess it doesn't."

Sunday's Colt

When Bill Sunday came riding down the lane on that spring day in 1910, Grandpa and I were standing at the corral fence watching the progress of Nan as she initiated another colt on a lesson of respect for the halter. Nan was a nineteen-year-old bay mule that Grandpa used exclusively for lead breaking colts. Yearling colts were haltered with the lead rope attached to a similar halter on the jenny. Nan and the colt were turned free in the corrals. When Nan wanted a drink, she went to water. When she became hungry, she went to the trough.

The colt had a choice as well. He could follow along, or he could kick, fight, bite, buck, balk, or throw himself...then follow along. Nan accepted such hysteric opposition with stoic strength, calmly waiting until her young companion learned that it was much easier to simply follow the jenny's lead. It seldom took more than an hour for the colt to resign himself to his situation.

We would monitor Nan and her colt for a while to make certain that the fighting didn't put the colt or the jenny in some type of dangerous predicament. The lead rope could get twisted around the colt's foreleg if he chose to strike at the jenny. The colt could throw himself and be unable to get to his feet. Or if he was especially strong, he might shake loose from his halter. Such situations seldom developed, but experience taught Grandpa that some caution should be exercised. Usually after a day or so of being tied to Nan, the worst young bronc became meekly submissive to the dictates of the halter.

Grandpa was seventy years old. We usually broke eight to ten horse or mule colts a month from early spring until late fall. He seldom took a chance with any of them. He liked to say that there were two ways to break a colt or filly—one method was with the back, the other with the brains. He took great pride in the fact that the vast majority of his colts were brought from halter to harness or saddle without the animal ever bucking or fighting. His methods became simple. He always gave the animal time to accept its circumstance and always put the animal in a situation where it had few options other than acceptance. He abhorred rough treatment, but he could be firm when it came time for a colt to accept his will. He liked to tell that he loved horses and mules from a professional perspective. Horses were neither pets nor friends, but tools. Only a greenhorn thought of them in any other way. An animal that could not be trusted had no value to a man who had to depend upon the beast for his livelihood. The more service an animal could render, the more value. He priced his livestock according to the amount of dependable service that he felt would be provided, and he seldom had stock on hand that was not spoken for. We worked hard and made a good living. O. C. Tate's horse and mule ranch had a national reputation. Grover Cleveland rode an O. C. Tate stallion to his inaugural.

I didn't notice the buckskin pinto colt that was slung across the pommel of Bill Sunday's saddle as he approached. Grandpa was twenty feet from Sunday when he stopped and sighed.

"Where did ya find him?" Grandpa asked.

Sunday centered the colt in his saddle and shook his head. "His mama took a lightning hit, I reckon. I found her in my pasture south of Seward. This little fellow was just waiting for her to wake up."

Grandpa tipped his weather-beaten Stetson to the back of his head and gave Sunday a disgusted look, "That storm was three days ago and this colt couldn't be more than five days old."

I stepped past Grandpa to get a closer look at the colt. He had a dandy head and was well marked. He was buckskin with black mane and tail, a nice white blaze pattern between his eyes, four white feet from the cannons down, and a white spot the general shape of South America on the upper right side of his withers. Other than some white patches scattered along his belly, he was regular buckskin.

"Got a lot of mustang in him from his daddy," Bill said softly as I examined the colt, "but his mom was pure thoroughbred. He won't be a tall horse, but I'm betting he'll be all guts when it comes to cow work."

"If you had an ounce of decency, Sunday, you'd have used that old Colt on him," Grandpa said as he pointed to the holstered, 32-20 single-action that old Bill habitually carried.

Sunday threw me one of those looks. His face said it all: Help me out, Andy. Say something to get me off the spot. He's going to tell me what a fool I am. I know the colt probably doesn't have a chance, but I just couldn't bring myself to put him under.

I could only shrug and mug a reply. "Don't look at me. I know exactly how you feel, but why should I look like a fool to save your face?"

"You ought to know better, Bill," Grandpa said. "That little feller doesn't have a snowball's chance in July!"

Sunday cast his eyes toward the small, white-frame house on the sandy knoll behind us. "I thought maybe Nell…"

Grandpa quickly looked over his shoulder to see if she was in sight before speaking. "Don't you get her involved in this. I know how that'll work. You'll ride off a-smiling and scratching; feeling like you did your bit while we'll get the pleasure of watching her sit up all night trying to save this orphan. Then we'll get to see the look on her face when we have to haul a dead colt from the kitchen. Meanwhile, you'll have forgotten all about the matter. Your conscience will be clear and her heart will be broken…again."

Sunday's eyes cut to mine. I shook my head and stared right back. He knew we were on to him.

Grandma called from the porch, "What you got there, Bill?"

The morning sun danced across her white hair as she stepped from the shadows.

Sunday smiled with relief. "I got me an orphan colt here, Nell. I thought maybe you might be able to do something to help him out."

"Bring him up to the house, Bill. I'll see if I can't get something down him," Grandma called before stepping through the screen door.

Grandma Tate was a tall woman, just a few inches shorter than Grandpa's six-foot frame. While Grandpa easily carried a big-shouldered two hundred and fifty pounds of bulk, she was thin and lanky. Her hair was cut short and so white that it drew your eyes to her in a crowd. Judging from the old tintype wedding portrait hanging on their bedroom wall, she had been a beauty in her youth—soft-featured, doe-eyed, and dark-haired.

Sunday immediately swung down from his gelding and lifted the colt from the saddle. He stepped by Grandpa in an arrogantly victorious fashion as he made his way toward the house.

"Your day's a-coming," Grandpa said as Sunday strolled toward the house.

Sunday was able to sneak a wink my way as he passed, juggling the mildly resisting colt in his arms.

"Andy, why don't you water Bill's gelding and tie him in the shade," Grandpa said as he followed Sunday toward the house.

I did as he told, checked the progress in the halter-breaking pen, and then rushed to the house. I found them gathered around the colt on the screened porch adjoining the front kitchen. Sunday had the colt by the neck, his rump wedged into the northwest corner while Grandma was gently coaxing the colt to try a little raw cow's milk from a rubber nipple stretched over the mouth of a milk bottle. The colt protested and balked until he got the first accidental taste of the milk.

Grandpa chuckled, "Look at that. He's really giving that nipple a once-over."

Grandma nodded and smiled. "I think this one just might make it. He's just hungry enough to accept the nipple and not so weak that he doesn't have the strength to suck."

When the colt had drained the bottle of its half-cup contents, Bill suggested that the colt could use some more.

"No," Grandma said firmly. "The worst thing you can do is give him too much too quickly. I'll give him another taste in an hour or so."

As Grandma withdrew the bottle, the colt strained against Bill's hold.

Grandpa chuckled at the colt's antics. At that moment I wondered if he had been so reluctant to accept the orphan because of the potential of Grandma's broken heart or his own. As I remember, it was always the two of them staying up all night, trying to save a colt or calf. In fact, it seemed as though Grandma took the death of the young animals a bit better than Grandpa. But no matter, I could always expect a day of quiet work and silent meals when a youngster didn't make it.

As Bill struggled to restrain him, the colt lurched forward as quick as a rifle shot and kicked the old cowboy in the shoulder. Bill lost his balance, falling back into the corner.

"Boy! That little feller's got a hair trigger!" Bill laughed as he rubbed his shoulder and regained his balance.

I grabbed the colt about the neck to hold him before he knocked Grandma from her feet as well. His tiny frame tensed at my touch and his strength was impressive. As I held the colt fast, I noticed the tiny white forehead marking resembling a lightning bolt.

"Lightning." I whispered as I gained control of my prize.

From that day forward, the colt had his name.

We had a bit of luck with the colt two days later. Grandpa showed up for breakfast and reported that Sally, a dark brown American saddle brood mare, had issued a stillborn filly during the night. Sally was an extremely protective mare and usually raised a fine colt. Although Grandpa felt that the bloodlines of the stillborn filly were better than Lightning's, he was thankful that we had the little buckskin to use as a replacement.

After our usual breakfast of fresh side bacon, eggs, fried potatoes, and biscuits, Grandpa and I made our way out to the corral to skin out the dead colt. I stopped by the buggy shed to retrieve a few lengths of binding twine. It was an unpleasant task to skin a stillborn colt or calf, but it was the surest method for getting a mother to adopt an orphan. By taking the hide from the sides and back of the dead animal and tying it to the orphan's back under the belly with binding twine, the mother's scent would be on the orphan. This usually aroused the mother's maternal instincts toward the foundling. Once the colt had cycled the adopted mother's milk through his system, the hide could be removed. By that time there was enough of the mother's scent on the orphan that she would continue to claim him. It was always an odd sight to see a young colt or calf wearing the crude hide jacket for his first encounter with his adoptive mother, but it usually worked, especially if the mother possessed strong maternal instincts as Sally did. The only other methods available were to try to catch the urine of the mare and pour it over the orphan or simply force an adoption. Forcing an adoption meant tying the mother in a stall and monitoring the sucking of the orphan. This was hard on the mother, orphan, and the people involved. It usually meant a daily fight for dominance, and since colts naturally nurse several times a day—grabbing a snack here and there when convenient—the procedure wasn't as natural and usually resulted in a bloat-bellied and underfed colt or calf. Neither method worked nearly as well as using the hide. Lightning was accepted immediately by his foster mother and we were able to remove his smelly jacket three days later. It wasn't long until a passer-by would doubt that the little buckskin wasn't the natural offspring of the tall brown.

Grandpa and Grandma had lived together for fifty years. They had raised five children to adulthood, all of them born on the ranch. They were married in Cottonwood Falls, Kansas in 1860, just before homesteading the rolling sandhills of central Kansas a hundred and fifty miles west. They went west in a covered wagon and settled into a sod dugout that was eventually used as the root cellar on the same sandy knoll where the house stood. Grandma liked to tell of those early years on the prairie. She told of how the young couple had faced down some drunken Indians with a shotgun on the journey out, and the year of the terrible prairie fire when they huddled together in the dugout as the horrendous blaze roared past them. There was the time in 1868 when an Indian uprising caused them to flee in their wagon with two infants to Fort Larned for protection. It was five years before they had a neighbor within five miles. I once asked Grandma if it was lonely during those early years. She said that she thought she was going to lose her mind a few times before the babies came. They would go for months without seeing another soul. She took to talking to herself just for some company. Once she had infants to care for, it wasn't nearly so bad.

The three oldest children, Glenn, Beryl, and Opal, were twenty years older than Delmar and Jean. Glenn had served in the military, rising to the rank of cavalry sergeant before taking a position as a Deputy U.S. Marshal in Missouri. Beryl had gone to work for the Atchison, Topeka, and Santa Fe railroad when he was sixteen and little had been heard from him after that. The last word from him had come from the Yukon during the gold rush of the 1890s. Rumor had it that he was in California. Opal had married a dry goods merchant from Larned where they prospered until he was killed in a horse wreck. She then married a homesteader who took her off to La Junta, Colorado. She wrote regularly, but the distance kept her fairly isolated.

Delmar was my father. He had remained on the ranch to partner up with Grandpa. He and my mother died during an influenza epidemic shortly after I was born. My Aunt Jean was married to the postmaster in St. John, twenty-five miles southeast. It took most of a day to get to the small settlement that had been built around the newly established Santa Fe railroad, but of all my aunts and uncles, it was Jean who maintained the most contact.

Living with my grandparents was the only life I knew. They had always been old. Our neighbors to the north, the Thairs, were old. Bill Sunday, a bachelor cowboy who ran a one-loop outfit to the east was old. The Porters, a black family of former slaves, lived two miles west. Ben Porter was a good farmer and we shared seasonal work—especially during harvest and hay cutting—but I had little dealings with his children who were mostly girls. I grew up with horses, mules, cattle, pigs, chickens, dogs, and guns. I went to Eden Valley School through the grades with the Porter girls and a strange kid named Curt O'Dell. Curt always seemed to be in a world of his own—quiet and sullen. He didn't finish school. My last year, it was just Polly and Edna Porter, their little brothers and sisters, and some younger children from some other homesteads. At fourteen years of age, I was out of school and ready to see the world. The only problem was that Grandpa and Grandma needed me. It was one thing for the oldest children to leave and go their separate ways, but that was thirty years earlier. They didn't say that I couldn't go. I'm sure they would have allowed me. It was just that I couldn't leave them. We had ranch hands and wranglers but none of them stayed for long. I was part of the ranch. I took pride in it and pride in myself for being a part of it. Even old Bill Sunday said that I was as good a wrangler at fourteen as he had ever seen. But then, when you're raised on the back of a horse, such talents would only come naturally. On the ground I was tall, big footed, and awkward.

I was also green. Other than our semi-annual trips to Larned to buy and sell stock, and irregular visits to St. John and Seward, I had little contact with the outside world. We sold grain at the Walnut Hill Mill, twenty miles north on the Arkansas River, and on special occasions we visited Great Bend. But for the most part, I worked horses and mules, did chores, and helped my grandparents. I worked hard, and to the best of my knowledge never lacked for anything. My prized possessions were my tall-crowned Stetson hat that my uncle Glenn gave me when I finished school, a Heiser Rocky Mountain Roper saddle that had been my father's, and an octagon-barreled .22 Winchester pump-action rifle. The little rifle was an eye catcher—nickel plated with extremely dark walnut woodwork. Grandpa bought it from a fellow in Seward who claimed he needed some seed money. Grandpa felt that it was more likely beer money, but the rifle was a bargain and I needed one to replace a worn out old single shot Stevens. I was never more than a few feet from the Winchester. As can probably be guessed, I seldom missed anything that I shot at.

Grandpa had two sections of grassland and a quarter section and eighty of farmland. We raised a little wheat, red cane, dry land corn, and alfalfa for the livestock. Grandpa built his cowherd up to a hundred head of Herefords and a few Jersey milking cows, which was a lot for those times in that area. He also raised mules and horses. He had twenty brood mares and a mammoth jack burro called Simplex that he bred to the mares. He also purchased unbroken colts for training. Sometimes we would have fifty head that needed to be broke. We also kept hogs, chickens, geese, turkeys, and ducks for home use. We always had at least one good border collie to help handle stock. Grandpa always named the dog Laddie. After a few years we got so we referred to dogs that had passed on as Laddie One, Laddie Four, or whatever number was appropriate. When Lightning came along, we were on Laddie Five. Laddie had always been a good name and Grandpa was superstitious about changing the name for fear he would get a chicken killer or egg sucker if he did.

Our day work was usually fairly regimented depending upon the season. We rose at sunrise and immediately fed the stock and milked the cows. A couple of hours later we ate breakfast and decided on the day's work. By eight or so we were in the fields or working livestock. By eleven we brought in the teams, fed, and watered them. We ate at noon, usually freshly killed fried chicken, boiled potatoes, and chicken gravy. We would usually rest for an hour after dinner—unless we were putting up hay or threshing wheat—before returning to the fields. By six o'clock, we would change teams or begin evening chores and milking. Depending upon the season and work to be done, we might eat our supper after chores and return to the fields, or call it a day. Grandpa always tried to keep a couple of men on during the farming season of spring, summer, and fall. They did most of the fieldwork while Grandpa handled the stock. During threshing season or hay harvest, we might have crews of twelve men, usually neighbors who shared work. I always enjoyed those times when we had big crews. We ate like kings, each woman at each homestead seemingly trying to outdo the others in preparing harvest meals. There was always lots of practical joking and good-natured conversation during those times. The days were long and the work hard, but the communal aspects made it fun.

Grandpa had a nice place but it wasn't anything special. We had an enormous barn that was the center of activity during the day. It was a gable-roofed affair with a loft and stalls on both sides of a center alleyway. "O. C. Tate Horses and Mules" was painted in black on the second story loft drop door. A hay grapple hung from the peak above the door. Hay was lifted from wagons to the loft and dumped with a pulley system that depended on a team of mules on the opposite end of the barn. When I was small, the grapple team was my responsibility. Later, I usually worked in the barn spreading and stacking the loose hay with a pitchfork. The barn was surrounded on three sides by rough plank corrals. To the south was the breaking corral where most of the horse work took place.

Between the working corral and the house was the wagon and tack shed—a ramshackle clapboard barn with large rolling doors. There was also a chicken house and a brooder house west of the tack shed. On the hill were Grandma's house and the washhouse with a windmill for pumping water. There was also a taller windmill in the stock corrals. Hog pens and the outhouses were west of the house at the base of the hill. They seemed to go with each other.

Because of a shortage of lumber on the prairie in the 1870s, the house was begun with a simple ten-by-twelve single room mail order package from Sears, Roebuck & Company. Most of our store-bought clothing came from orders made from the Sears, Roebuck catalog. Later, another room of similar size was added, and still later a twenty-by-twenty square foot addition was added to the east. Grandma had finally got her screened porch at the north end of the original building that functioned as a kitchen after the turn of the century. Behind the house to the south was the cement root cellar that was poured over the original dugout—a flower garden and vegetable patch. Grandma always worked in the gardens in the early morning when it was cool. There was also a small windmill beside the root cellar that kept a constant supply of cool water circulating through the concrete cooling and storage tanks, and supplied irrigation water for the gardens. Fresh milk and eggs were stored in the cooling tanks, as well as canned goods arranged on wooden shelves along three walls. Circling the house on all sides were young cottonwood trees that had been planted in the 1890s. Four American elms also grew near the house at all four points of the compass. A small orchard of pear, cherry, and green apple trees was south of the gardens. There was also a clump of cottonwoods east of the barn where most of the repair work to wagons and machinery was done in the shade.

During the day, the place resounded with the frantic sounds of braying mules, cackling chickens and geese, gobbling turkeys, cattle calls, pig squeals, windmill pumping, hammering and repairing, and men working livestock. In the evening it was quiet, usually only disturbed by the ever-present mechanical clattering of the windmills, house activities, and the nearly constant wind singing through the cottonwoods. Sitting on the porch in the cool of the evening was my favorite time of day during the summer. After a long day's work it was pleasant to just relax on the porch with a glass of lemonade or tea made from fresh well water. Grandpa would usually smoke a pipe of tobacco and rock in his rocking chair as he waited for Grandma to finish supper dishes. I loved the sweet, heavy, and overpowering odor of his pipe smoke. Finally, Grandma would join him in her rocker. After thirty minutes or so, I would get my cue to head for bed. They would remain on the porch for an hour longer.

I often wondered what they talked about during that private time on those late summer evenings. Was it about crops, livestock, plans for the future, or memories of the past? Sometimes I would lie in bed and try to hear the conversation, but the sounds were always too far away to make sense. Every once in a while I would remember something that I felt I needed to bring to their attention before I fell asleep. I would get up and make my way to the porch in the dark to pass on the information. Invariably, they would be holding hands when I stepped through the door.

Lightning matured to become a fine strong cow pony under the protection of his foster mother. As the colt developed, we could expect periodic visits from Bill Sunday. Bill would usually ride in unannounced, spend a few minutes talking with Grandpa about livestock or farming, then casually ask about the colt. This request would always result in a walk to the corrals or horse pasture so Bill could get a look at the colt. Bill would nod his head, comment on the colt's progress, and then make some statement concerning Lightning's ancestry. Bill usually observed that there would not be another horse with the same breeding. Bill planned to breed several good mares to a mustang stud with the idea of eventually selling good cow ponies. He bought a dune mustang from a Comanche Indian in Oklahoma because he had been impressed with the animal's strength, endurance, and temperament. Lightning's mother had been the highest priced mare Bill had ever purchased. He chose her because of her thoroughbred bloodline and looks. The old stud died shortly after he serviced the mare and before any of Bill's other mares were ready. The lightning strike on the mare ended the plan completely. Only the little buckskin remained to give Bill any indication of whether his plan had been sound.

Bill had a good eye for horses, and his predictions of how the grown colt would look were correct. Lightning grew to become a short thickset horse barely fourteen hands tall. He had long silky hair growing from behind his fetlocks and the heavy unruly mane typical of his mustang father. His ears were narrow and short; his nostrils narrow. These were all traits of the Spanish ancestry characteristic of mustangs.

From his mother he inherited a finely chiseled head, large handsome eyes, and thickset heart girth. He was a full two hands shorter than his foster mother and his neck at least two inches thicker. Bill felt that with his short thick stature, quick speed, and strength, the pony ought to be perfect for roping and cutting work.

Grandpa wasn't as impressed. He was of the school preferring tall horses. He complained that Lightning was more the size of a mule rather than a "real" horse. He reluctantly conceded that the little buckskin was awfully "showy" and certainly as quick-footed as any animal he had seen. The two old cowboys would often spend a few minutes debating the qualities of the colt before returning to the house for a glass of tea or fresh well water.

Everyone paid special attention to the colt. Even Grandma, who usually paid little attention to such matters, would occasionally take a walk in the pasture to check on the colt. I usually spent a quarter hour or so fooling with the colt every morning. Laddie always accompanied me. I tried to have a bit of apple, a handful of grain, or a little sugar robbed from Grandma's pantry for Lightning.

The colt would usually come running to me, his mother calmly watching warily from a distance. Playful and skittish, Lightning would usually run toward me at a full gallop, then throw on the brakes at the last instant. He would eagerly accept my treats but always with a close eye on my hands and the dog, sweeping away suddenly if he felt I was getting just a bit too close. He would jump and pitch as he turned away, often with an excited squeal that always brought his foster mother to attention. He never went very far though; always eager to be as independent as possible, but never so far that he might forfeit some goody that I might still have to offer. He would stand apart from me facing away, showing his rump, but always watching my actions. Eventually after demonstrating the proper degree of independence, he would casually turn about and return to my offerings. There would always be time for the morning nose touch of greeting with the collie—a cautious but friendly recognition of each other's presence.

Then as quick as a flash, he was off to the mare. Laddie was usually eager to give chase, but a word from me held him back. Although Sally was never very happy with the presence of the dog, Laddie and the colt could often be found renewing acquaintances in the horse pasture. There was something about the colt's antics that fascinated the collie. Both seemed enthralled with the other's strange appearance. They became comfortable companions. In the heat of the afternoon, Laddie could often be found resting in the shade of an old elm tree in the pasture, the colt usually nearby or resting beside him. Generally, Sally tolerated their unusual friendship with mild disapproval.

Grandpa and Bill made the decision early to geld the colt. Both felt that he would be of more value as a gelding rather than as a stud. Breeders would have little interest in Lightning's unique bloodline. Bill did not feel that the colt would be able to carry out his plan for a new type of horse. When Lightning turned two, it became time for him to get his education. His halter-breaking session with Nan was uneventful, but his first experience with the saddle was not smooth. In spite of the fact that he had spent a full day and night snubbed closely to the center post of the breaking corral before the attempt was made, the feisty colt did not take well to presence of the heavy breaking saddle. He puffed up and attempted to kick free of the halter and the saddle. He went to his knees in a vain attempt to roll the foreign object from his back. Grandpa had tied the halter rope too closely to the post for him to make a roll. The colt groaned in anger and sullenly refused to move or get back to his feet. Grandpa patiently suggested that we give him a few hours to come to terms with his bondage before attempting a ride.

By that evening, the colt had been twenty-four hours without water or feed. When we returned he was standing at the center post, resigned to the saddle on his back. I untied him and led him to the stock tank. He followed calmly and drank his fill. He also eagerly accepted a green apple that I had procured from Grandma's orchard.

The following morning I saddled up Old Ben—one of Grandpa's better riding horses—and led the saddled colt on a brisk five-mile workout. When we returned, the colt was sweaty and tired. Grandpa always preached that a colt learned best when he was exhausted and the fight gone. Before the colt had time to regain his strength, we slipped on a hackamore, tightened the cinch of the breaking saddle, and led him into the bucking pen. Grandpa slipped an old saddle blanket over the colt's eyes as I swung into the bear-trap bucking saddle. Grandpa used the unusual Flynn saddle for all preliminary breaking work. This saddle had a very wide swell that swept backward from the horn so a rider was literally in a trap between the high-back cantle and the backward fork. It was excellent for staying in the saddle, but almost impossible to get out of should the horse fall with the rider. Bill Sunday considered it a dangerous device and often commented that Grandpa should retire it to the barn. The saddle had been instrumental in my breaking my leg when a sorrel mare threw herself with me the preceding year. I still liked the Flynn for breaking because once I was set in the seat it was nearly impossible for a horse to throw me. After the experience with the sorrel, however, I was much more wary of a horse throwing himself.

Lightning humped up and threatened to pitch but he was too confused and tired to go through with it. While his crude blindfold was still in place, Grandpa led him around the pen several times until he became familiar with the weight on his back. After I gathered up the reins of the hackamore so the colt could not get his head down to buck, Grandpa gently slipped the blanket from his eyes.

"Now, keep his head up and watch your legs," Grandpa quietly suggested as he slipped the blanket free. "I wouldn't be surprised if he chose to throw himself."

I nodded and braced my thighs into the exaggerated swells of the bear-trap saddle. I wasn't eager to spend another winter on crutches and was ready to bail off if I suspected the colt would throw himself.

As Grandpa backed cautiously away, Lightning froze and trembled with uncertainty.

"Make him go," Grandpa said softly.

I relaxed a bit against the saddle to see if that would set the colt off. I waited a few seconds, then gently prodded his flanks with the heels of my boots. I never wore spurs when breaking a horse. The colt humped up again in confusion but did not move.

"He's going to be stubborn," Grandpa said as he took hold of the hackamore under the colt's chin.

Grandpa gently increased the forward force and tried to lead the colt as I gently prodded Lightning in the flanks. Lightning took a faltering step forward, then another, and another. Grandpa let go of the hackamore and allowed him to pass by. The colt kept on walking in a circle around the center post of the pen, staying a safe distance from the surrounding corral fence.

We made one circle around the post before Grandpa ordered, "Make him trot."

I nodded and braced myself against the fork of the saddle, squaring my rump into the high-backed cantle of the bear-trap saddle. At this point of a first ride, there was never a certainty of how a colt would react to the heel pressure on his flanks. Some went into a trot, some would balk, but a few would blow up underneath the rider.

Lightning puffed up and gave serious consideration to throwing a fit as I increased the pressure of my heels. After a bit of coaxing, he changed his mind and broke into his faster gait. Following a couple more circles around the pen at the trot, Grandpa nodded his head approvingly and ordered a halt.

I drew back the reins slowly until the colt came to a stop. He seemed to be resigned to my presence and showed little inclination to fight my commands.

"What do you think?" Grandpa asked as he stepped to the colt and took hold of the hackamore.

"He's ready," I answered. "Turn him out."

"Why don't you ride him over to Bill's," Grandpa said as he softly stroked Lightning on the neck with his free hand. "He'd like to see the colt being ridden and it's about the right distance for a first ride."

I nodded and patted Lightning's neck. Grandpa stepped away and opened the heavy swinging gate of the breaking corral. As I rode the colt across the farmyard I caught sight of Grandma standing next to the yard fence.

"Looks like he decided to be a gentleman," Grandma called.

"I think so."

"Watch him. He's quick coupled enough to throw you before you know what's happening," Grandpa said.

I nodded and waved to both of them as we made our way down the lane. Lightning seemed glad to be free of the pen, even if he was packing his unfamiliar load. We went down the lane easily and made the turn onto the road.

On the way to Bill's, I alternated the colt's gaits from walk to trot to gallop. He pitched the first time we broke into gallop but it was a half-hearted effort.

Lightning carried himself nicely. He was a smooth gaited two-year-old with a short neck. I could easily see why he would work well as a roping and cow pony. A high-headed horse was something of a bother when trying to manage a roping loop, and Lightning kept his head low and set forward.

By the time we reached Bill Sunday's place, he was pretty tired. Grandpa firmly believed that a horse didn't really begin learning anything until it was too tired to fight. He also believed that any colt that wasn't allowed to buck during his early training was unlikely to buck after being finished. The tactic didn't always work, but in Lightning's case it proved correct. After that first day, he never bucked no matter how difficult his circumstances.

Sunday was waiting in the yard for my visit. He smiled as I approached his two-room cabin. "Looks like you've worked him out nicely."

I leaned forward over the saddle horn and stroked Lightning's neck. "He's done real well."

"Step down, Andy. Let's give him a breather before you start back."

I eased to the ground and led him to Bill's watering tank. Bill and I led him to the shade of a large cottonwood that grew next to the cabin.

Being a Texan, Bill was of the habit of squatting over his knees rather than sitting on the ground. He squatted and began rolling himself a cigarette from the makings he carried in his shirt pocket.

"What do you think of him?" he asked matter-of-factly as I sat on the ground next to him.

"I think he'll be all right."

Sunday struck a match against the handle of his old Colt and lit his cigarette. "Your grandpa and I are sorta partners on this feller. We talked it over the other day and decided that if you liked him, the horse ought to be yours."

"You think so?"

"Yeah. I'd hate to see him sold and we both think you need a horse of your own."

"Thanks, Bill. I think that would be all right,"

"There is one condition," Bill said after taking another puff on his cigarette.

"What's that?"

"I think that after you've broke him to the lariat and got him cattle wise, some feller's going to offer you quite a price for him. I'm asking that you don't sell him, no matter what you're offered. Hell, if you need to...to get yourself off the spot...tell that feller he's Bill Sunday's colt and you can't sell him."

Of course I wouldn't sell the colt. It was funny that the old cowboy had thought up some tactic for me to keep from selling Lightning no matter how tempting the offer.

"I'll tell you what, Bill. As far as anyone's concerned he's Sunday's colt. We'll just be partners on him. How's that?"

Bill put out his hand to seal the deal. "That would be fine, partner. That would be just fine."

During the course of the following year we turned Lightning into a solid roping horse. Although we didn't do as much roping as the large outfits farther west, it was important that we had horses that knew the work. Pink eye was a problem in the summer. Hoof rot was an ailment demanding immediate care. Cows in trouble during calving season in the spring had to be caught. A roping horse needed to be able to hold a calf while it was being doctored. Roping demanded speed, intelligence, and strength.

It wasn't the custom to dally rope. Dally roping was a practice developed by the Mexican vaqueros using forty-foot braided leather lariats and large rawhide-covered saddle horns. Once a vaquero roped an animal, he wrapped the end of his lariat around the saddle horn and either took up or let out slack as the situation demanded. This saved on the lariat and preserved the weak saddle frame. We tied our lariats hard and fast to smooth steel saddle horns. The saddles weren't designed for taking a quick wrap with our twenty-foot hemp lariats. Much of our roping was done in sandhills laced with plumb thickets and willows. There wasn't time to make a dally wrap after catching a calf. Our saddles were heavy with two cinches—one in front and another at the back—to keep them from tipping forward when the lariat went tight after a catch. The saddles featured high cantles, heavy swells at the fork, large square skirts, and wide fenders. The stirrups were often iron rather than wood. My Heiser weighed over forty pounds and was designed for heavy roping and dragging. Wrecks were not common but could happen if a calf veered off at an angle before the rope was tight, or managed to get a tree or bush between the horse and itself after a catch. For this reason we often had a strap with the lariat fed between it and the horse's neck to keep a newly trained pony's head in line with the calf after the catch. It didn't take long for a horse to learn to keep the lariat at an angle of the best advantage. Lightning excelled under the lariat. He was quick enough to get in close and stay with the calf. He was also solid enough to take the heavy pounding of the force of catching a calf—and he liked it. Some horses never do take well to being tied to a fighting calf; others seem to enjoy the power over another animal. Lightning was that kind of horse. Old timers called such horses "cow wise."

A good rider, however, seldom threw his pony to a dead stop as is commonly seen in modern rodeo calf-roping events. It was much wiser to draw the pony to a slow stop, easing the stress on the saddle, horse, and calf's neck. "Busting" cattle wasn't tolerated. Grandpa said that cattle with broken or crooked necks didn't turn much of a profit.

We seldom roped full-sized cows unless we had one that wouldn't stay home. Roping bulls was usually out of the question unless there were several riders to get a loop on him. We had one old Hereford bull named Jiggs that gave us a show. Jiggs was a swept-horned giant weighing close to a ton. This old boy was wise to cowboys and lariats and always seemed to be interested in cows and heifers in other pastures. That first year working Lightning, we lost track of the bull about mid-summer. That fall, a farmer from Seward stopped by to ask us if we were missing a bull with a broken bar T brand. He had been spotted along the Mystery River in a thick stand of willows and cottonwoods. The locals had tried to catch Jiggs but had little luck, no one feeling competent to lay a loop on him. The Mystery River was an underflow creek that came to the surface during wet years. A person could follow its course because of surrounding timber stands drawing moisture from the underground water. The course was too boggy for farming and was ideal for young trees to take root. Farmers on foot were not able to drive the bull or catch him in the soft ground surrounding the Mystery's course.

Knowing we would probably have a tussle with the bull, Grandpa asked Bill Sunday and a couple of local cowboys to help us. Dan Scott and Jack Pearson were older than I was by a few years and fancied themselves quite the bronc busters. Five riders pulled out of our place on a cold October Saturday morning. Dan had a seven-foot bullwhip to drive the bull into the open where we could get a loop on him if it was necessary. The farmers complained that old Jiggs would fight every time anyone got near him. If a bull wouldn't submit to herding, a man on foot was at his mercy.

We hadn't ridden a mile before Dan and Jack were criticizing Lightning's size. The cowboys said the colt was too little for me…that I ought to be riding a "real" horse, and they hoped he wouldn't be played out before we got to Seward. Of course this good-natured teasing didn't sit well with Bill Sunday. He listened sullenly before offering a dollar bet that Lightning would still be going when the other horses were played out. Being self-styled vaqueros, the pair jumped at the bet. Grandpa said that he hoped we didn't kill a horse that day to settle a two-dollar bet.

After talking to the farmer, we began a sweep of the river to locate the bull. Grandpa spotted Jiggs first as he broke from a wheat field. He was making tracks for a three-acre wilderness of willows and vines. Dan and Jack dug in their spurs and fired their horses into the trees after him. By the time Grandpa, Bill, and I arrived, the cowboys were riding the edges looking for tracks. They could find no sign of the bull and figured he had hot-footed it down the river course.

Bill suggested a sweep through the trees to make sure the bull hadn't been missed. Dan complained that it was just a bit difficult to miss a ton bull in a three-acre patch of trees. Grandpa, however, overruled them saying that it was best to cover the ground as well as possible. Old Jiggs was a lot craftier than most and Grandpa didn't relish the idea of passing the bull if he could prevent it.

We made the sweep through the trees, keeping each other in sight. There seemed to be no sign of the bull in the tangled undergrowth. As we passed through, the cowboys suggested that Jiggs must have made his way down the river.

"Show me the tracks!" Bill said.

Grandpa ordered a second unsuccessful sweep of the trees with no success. A cold rain began under low-rolling clouds. We spread out, making our way down the river course looking for tracks or some sign of the wayward bull. After four miles of searching, Grandpa decided that we must have missed that bull or the tracks where he had travelled across open cropland on either side. We wheeled about and started working our way back. I broke off from the group and rode to the crest of a nearby hill to see if I could spot the bull from a distance. The other riders left me behind. I was in no hurry to catch up. Somebody must have missed some sign of the bull. I was a half-mile behind when they entered the three-acre grove. By the time I reached the grove, they were through it and sweeping the upstream course of the river. I spotted old Jiggs in the grove following the riders. How he had managed to hide himself will always be a mystery.

I drew up Lightning, shook out a loop, and gave a war cry, "Here he is!"

The old bull spun around, gave me a mean-eyed glare, and broke for the open. Being seventeen years old—cocky and immortal—I set Lightning in lone pursuit of a bull that outweighed the pair of us by eight hundred pounds.

I was on the bull within a quarter of a mile. Lightning drew in on his tail and I gave my lariat a side-handed pitch. The loop curled around Jiggs's shoulder and circled over his horns. It was a nearly perfect throw—the kind a fellow always manages when no one is around to see it. I slowly drew back and allowed the slack to work out of the rope so Lightning wasn't jerked off his feet. Jiggs felt the lariat about his horns and turned to face me. Jiggs trembled in anger at the end of the lariat. I called to the others for help. I wasn't sure how long we would maintain the standoff and there was no nearby tree to tie the bull off.

Several minutes passed as I kept the lariat tight against the bull's horns. I glanced about to try to see the others. When the bull took a step forward, I'd back Lightning to regain the slack. Suddenly, Jiggs came at us in a full-blown charge. I flipped up the rope to clear the pony's feet and set off at a run to angle away from the bull and bring my rope tight again. Once we came tight, I wheeled Lightning about and drew him to a stop. Again, old Jiggs bucked and fought against the lariat.

We repeated the ritual several more times as the bull worked us into a small stand of willows. I kept calling to try to get some kind of help. No one seemed to be hearing. We were pinned against a clump of sandhill plumb thickets and the bank of a small creek. Old Jiggs came in too quickly for us to work out of the spot and got his head under Lightning's belly. With a mighty heave, the bull lifted us off the ground and dumped us head-over-heels into the thicket.

I struggled to get free of the saddle. Luckily, the bushes were thick enough that they held Lightning's weight off my leg. I slipped the rope from the saddle horn. Jiggs went for the tree cover, leaving us to get free of the thickets. I managed Lightning to his feet and looked him over. He was trembling and sweaty but I could find no other damage. I was thankful he wasn't hurt.

The others came charging by. Grandpa drew up his horse and asked if I was all right.

"Yeah, it wasn't as bad as I thought," I answered without looking up.

"Is that so?" Grandpa asked as he pointed to the thickets behind me. "Then why is your spur hanging in that plumb bush?"

I glanced over my shoulder to see my right spur dangling in the fork of the bush we had just crawled from. I turned back toward Grandpa as he gave me a look of mild disapproval.

"You better be more careful. You'll get yourself killed pulling stunts like that."

Before I could answer he set out in pursuit of the others. I examined Lightning's condition again to make sure I had not missed anything and replaced the spur.

Things hadn't gone well during my absence. Dan tried a loop and missed. A second later, Jack managed a similar miss. Bill Sunday then swung in to throw his loop just as the bull drove into the water of the little creek. His rope caught, but he had a bull to fight in the middle of the water with no sure footing for his horse. It was a steep bank and none of the others could close in enough to throw a second loop. Bill let the bull have his head and followed him up the other side of the bank.

As Bill came up the opposite bank, his horse lost footing and fell backward into the creek. The slack on the rope tightened and jerked Bill's saddle around to his horse's belly. Both slid along a mud bank, unable to get to their feet or free from the bull. Bill drew his pocketknife and cut the rope.

When I came up to the bank, only Bill was left refitting his saddle and examining his horse. Both were covered with the mud of the bank.

"Heck of a rodeo, ain't it?" he said quietly.

"No kidding. Where did they go?"

"Off toward the trees. You better hurry. Your grandpa is going to need some help. Them five-and-dime cowboys can't lasso worth a damn."

"You all right?"

Bill cut his eyes to mine and smiled. "Just getting old, Andy. I should have known better than to have tried that stunt."

"I should have known better myself, Bill," I said as I passed.

"Yeah, but you got an excuse. You're just a kid. An old man like me should have picked a better spot than this mud bath."

I didn't answer. Bill had hurt his pride and didn't need unappreciated comfort from me.

As I approached the trees I could hear the breaking of limbs and bushes as the riders and old Jiggs battled. Jiggs charged out of the trees in my direction—Grandpa hot on his tail—swinging his loop. The old bull had two lariats draped off his horns, dragging behind him. Forty feet out from the trees Grandpa let fly, and the loop settled over the bull's neck. As he drew the rope tight, Jiggs spun about and balked. I jumped to the ground, grabbed the closest rope, and climbed back into the saddle. I finished retying just as Jiggs decided to charge Grandpa. Caught between two tight lines from opposite ends, the bull could do little. Dan and Jack threw their loops over the bull's horns. Our four horses were able to drag the unruly Hereford toward the ranch. Jiggs was unhappy but shortly gave up the struggle. By the time we reached the barn Jiggs was too exhausted to put up any more fight.

Bill wasn't. He said it seemed odd that neither Jack nor Dan could seem to place a rope on that bull until someone else had managed it. He wondered aloud if either of them had been to the eye doctor lately since they had ridden right over the top of a ton bull without seeing him. He observed that Indians had always liked horses like they were riding because they could always catch them when afoot. He spent at least fifteen minutes pointing out the qualities of Lightning and how he always figured he'd pick a short horse any day over the three-legged crowbaits that others seemed to be riding lately.

It was merciless. I could almost see the cowboys ducking Bill's verbal blows. Bill sent them packing after we freed the bull in the breaking corral. He started in on how good that beer was going to taste when he collected those dollar bets. They left sullenly without a word.

I never learned whether Bill collected those bets. Even if he didn't, I know he got way more than two dollars worth of revenge before we managed the bull back to the pens.

Early April of 1914, Grandpa made the decision to replace Simplex. The old jack was getting old and good mules were a large part of our income. Grandpa spent most of the winter trying to locate a jack with just the right qualities. He wanted a black at least fourteen hand high that could sire mules of similar color. Tall black mules were extremely popular with the army and farmers. A possible war in Europe meant higher prices for good stock.

Grandpa had a second cousin living on a ranch north of Grand Island, Nebraska, who had just such a young jack for sale. From Jed

Groves's description and a Kodak photograph, Grandpa figured he would gamble on purchasing the jack. It was spring planting and auction season, however, and Grandpa didn't feel he had the time to make the long journey to Grand Island. He asked Bill Sunday to accompany me for final inspection and purchase. I jumped at the opportunity. It was my chance to see some of the world. In return for a modest fee and Grandpa's promise to monitor his place while he was absent, Sunday agreed to go.

Grandpa gave me with a bank draft and expense money. Bill and I would be gone at least three weeks—the longest period of time I would ever be absent up to that time. So, packing supplies in our saddlebags and bedrolls on our horses, Bill and I set out for the ride to Nebraska.

I learned a lot about Bill Sunday during that trip. Bill was a wiry old cowboy well into his seventies and had an exciting life during the development of the West. Bill looked every inch the Texas cowboy of the old days. He sported a huge walrus mustache that draped over his upper lip and hung down the sides of his mouth. Although a bachelor all his life, Bill took pride in his appearance. His white collarless shirts were always bleached clean. He preferred high, stovetop, fancy-stitched boots with his pant legs worn inside and Texas style spurs with rowels as big around as a teacup. He wore a high-crowned, wide-brimmed Stetson hat and never felt completely dressed without a large colorful bandana tied loosely around his neck. Although packing a sidearm was out of fashion by the turn of the century, Bill habitually carried an old ivory-handled Colt. He usually left it in his saddlebags in town to avoid uncomfortable stares from townsfolk.

Bill came from Texas in the 1870s working the trail drives to Dodge City. His father had been a Confederate soldier who never returned from the war. His mother remarried a man with several children of his own and Bill set off to be a cowboy when he was only twelve years old. Cattle prices crashed at the end of the 1870s, ending the era of the long drives, and Bill took on work for local cattlemen. After a few years, he drifted to Stafford County and homesteaded a small place south of Seward. For years he had been Grandpa's closest neighbor and best friend.

Bill was a quiet man of simple pleasures. Other than an occasional glass of beer and a few games of dominos during infrequent trips to town, Bill preferred to stay home and work his small spread in solitude. He was short-spoken and opinionated concerning livestock and politics but seemed rather quiet when around anyone other than Grandpa. He was much more social with my grandparents. He would often spend long hours in the evenings joking and playing table games. I always liked Bill and listened intently when he offered advice. Other than my grandfather, he seemed to know more about horses and mules than any man I knew. He had a strict sense of honor. He had no use for a man whose word could not be trusted.

Bill couldn't read. When his business dealings demanded a written contract, he never signed it until he had Grandma read and explain it to him. He would often question her about meanings or phrases. He often said that Grandma was the best legal counsel in the country as far as he was concerned.

We reached Jed Groves's place nine days after leaving home. The ranch was similar to Grandpa's except it was nestled in the sandhills of Nebraska. When we rode into the place we were greeted by Jed's daughters. June was my age and outweighed me by fifty pounds. The second daughter, Jane, was odd and something of a crybaby. Jenny was seven years younger than Jane. She was dark-haired, tall, and thin like Grandma when she was young. I liked Jenny for her quiet ways and simple manner. I watched her often trying not to be obvious.

The jack that we had come for was everything Jed Groves claimed. He was named Black Jack. He was taller and heavier than Simplex and possessed excellent conformation and temperament for a jackass. Although I was impressed I didn't want to make a commitment until I had Bill's impressions. Bill stated bluntly that he had never seen a mammoth jack as good.

After a hectic two-day visit we started back to the ranch leading Black Jack. After a few miles I realized I was going to miss those girls. It was the first time that I had been around a family with so many children the same age as myself.

We stopped at Grand Island to see a vaudeville show. A fellow named Eddie Foy was performing. Bill said he had quite a reputation as a comedian. There were singers, dancers, and some quite attractive women on the stage. Foy was entertaining but he had unusually odd mannerisms. I thought it was strange that any man would act so foolish in front of a crowd. Bill said Foy reminded him of a Negro comedian he had seen on a riverboat show in Missouri when he was about my age.

I saw my first automobiles while in Grand Island. There were several Stanley Steamers and a Winton Flyer. I was especially impressed with a small white Buick parked in front of a hardware store. It was laced with brass ornamentation and had black leather pleated seats as fine as the fanciest buggy. It even had a mirror mounted on the dashboard so a driver could see what was behind him. Bill's only comment was that he couldn't see why any man would purchase such an expensive extravagance. He figured he would have to sell everything he owned just to buy one of the silly contraptions.

We also stopped at an implement dealership to look at a new Baldwin Brothers combine harvester.

"Just think of it, Andy," Bill said. "A fellow can do all of the jobs of a binder and steam thrashing machine with only one or two men. From standing crop to grain all in one operation."

I wasn't nearly as impressed. All that meant was an end to thrashing crews and all the fun of being with all those guys. It would be just like Grandpa to buy one of those things so we could be isolated during harvest as well.

That night, as we camped along the Platte River, Bill asked me if something was bothering me. I thought of all I had seen while I rubbed down Lightning and could only shake my head.

Finally, Bill spoke. "It's a big old world, isn't it?"

"Yeah, I guess it is."

"A young fellow like you would probably like to see more of it, wouldn't he?"

"I don't know. I've got a good life with Grandpa and Grandma. I don't know where I'd go if I had the chance."

"But?"

I went to the campfire for a cup of his coffee. "It's just that when you were younger than me, you had seen so much more of the world. You know…Texas, Indians, Missouri riverboat shows, girls and such. Grandpa and Grandma have seen things. About all I know about is the ranch, Seward, and St. John. That isn't much."

"Why don't you do something about it?"

"I've thought about it. I thought about joining the cavalry like my Uncle Glenn. Or go to Alaska or somewhere like Uncle Beryl."

"What's stopping you?" Bill sipped his coffee.

"You know. I can't leave them alone. What would they do without me? Grandpa isn't getting any younger. Who would break his horses for him?"

"Your grandpa isn't a poor man. He could afford to hire a hand."

I stared into the fire. "What do you think I should do?"

Bill pitched the leavings from his cup into the fire and poured a fresh helping of coffee. "It isn't for me to say. It isn't for your grandparents to say either. You're eighteen years old. That's a decision for a man to make and you're a man. Your grandparents see it that way as well."

"They've said something?"

"They've talked on it some. It was your Grandma's suggestion that you take this trip. She thought it would be a good idea for you to get out and meet Jed Groves's daughters."

"What in the world for?"

"The two oldest girls are about marrying age."

"Good Grief! What in the world would I want to get married for? And especially to one of those girls! June would make two of me. And besides, you never got married."

"Well, I hope to John that you don't plan on modeling your life after mine!" Bill said, choking on his coffee.

"Why not? You got all you need. You've got a nice little place. You make out."

"I don't have anyone like your grandmother. She's as fine and kind a woman as I've ever known. O. C. was a lucky man the day he met up with the likes of her."

"Do you miss it?"

"Most of the time, no. But then, there are times when I do. I get to thinking that it would be awful nice to have a lady to take with me to town or to visit your grandparents. Things can get pretty lonely during those long winter nights when all you got is your chores and yourself for company."

He was quiet for a while. "And then there's children. Who's going to be around for me to give my place to when I'm gone? Who's going to miss me when I ain't around anymore?"

"We'll all miss you."

"I know that. But it ain't the same. It ain't like having blood kin. For all I know, I'm the only Sunday left. Don't get me wrong. I've had a good life and I've got few regrets. It's just that a man should think about such things when he's your age. A woman like your grandma could be quite a comfort as the years pass."

"Excuse me if I try to do better than June Groves."

Bill shook out his bedroll. "Well, she would be nice on those cold winter nights."

"We could always go back and see if she's interested in hitching up with you."

Bill crawled into his bedroll and pulled his hat over his eyes. "If I was twenty years younger, we might just do that."

I watched Bill for several moments wondering if he was serious. "Good night, Bill," I finally said.

"Good night, Andy."

I thought about what Bill said as I waited for sleep. I watched Lightning, hobbled and grazing nearby. I could see a lot of the world from the back of my buckskin. I could go to Wichita or Kansas City. Or, I could go to Texas. Now that was an idea. I could ride down to Texas and even see the Gulf of Mexico. Or maybe I could go to California and see the orange groves. I could take on short-time work as a cowboy on different spreads and see the whole West in a couple of years. I could join the Army; perhaps fight in a war in Cuba or against the Kaiser in Europe. But then I'd have to leave Lightning with my grandparents, and I'd have to leave the ranch. What would they do without me? What would I do without them? Oh, they'd be all right. They'd do just fine. Grandpa could hire another man to help out. Then I would be free to see the world.

Lightning was grazing within a foot or so from my head. I sat up and fished a bit of sugar from my saddlebags. He took my offering and I gently stroked the side of his head.

"What do you think, Lightning?"

He nudged my hand begging for more sugar. I pushed him away. He couldn't care less, I thought. He had it easy. He didn't have to worry about such things. He worked his way into the darkness and I relaxed in my bedroll. Perhaps I would say something to Grandpa and Grandma when we got back to the ranch.

Bill rolled over in his bedroll onto his side. I thought about what he had said about my grandmother. What would the world be like without her? It would be pretty lonely.

There were a lot of stars out that night. It was a big world and I had seen only a very small part of it, but the part of the world I knew was good. That night I dreamed of fat wives, vaudeville shows, and trading Lightning for a new Buick that wouldn't run.

Black Jack turned out to be everything we had hoped. He sired such fine mules that many farmers brought in their own horses for him to breed. Grandpa had flyers printed to advertise the jack's availability for stud. Prices were high for everything we sold during those years. Grandpa said that they were the best years that he had ever seen. The high market was the result of the war that raged in Europe.

Other things did not go so well the summer of 1915. Grandma would say the same things several times a day. She would forget to prepare meals or work in the garden for hours on end at odd times of the day. She would become frustrated or deny doing things that only she could have done. Grandpa didn't say much at first but finally decided she needed to see a doctor. He took her to Great Bend to get the best professional advice. The doctor's diagnosis was simple. Grandma was rapidly becoming senile. There was nothing to be done. I remember the tears in Grandpa's eyes when he told me. For the first time he seemed at a loss for a solution to a problem. Of course, my plans to go off on my own were forgotten.

Aunt Jean stayed with us for a while but she had children and responsibilities of her own. She offered to take Grandma to live with her but Grandpa would have none of that. He insisted that she remain in her home where she wouldn't be frightened or confused. Grandpa attempted to get one of the Porter girls to stay with us, but one had gone to Kansas City to work and the other was about to marry a fellow from Hoisington. We struggled through the winter and the following spring attempting to take care of her and the household chores.

June 13, 1915, was a terrible day. It was miserably hot and Grandpa was doctoring sick pigs. I was out checking cattle on Lightning. I found a break in a fence and by the time I had gathered up stray stock and made the necessary repairs it was two in the afternoon before I was able to get back. When I returned, Grandpa was nowhere to be found. After some searching, I found him in the west pasture, on foot, following Grandma's tracks. He was nearly frantic. Grandma's condition had become so bad that she would forget to eat or drink enough fluids. Grandpa carried her bonnet. He was especially concerned that she would collapse from sunstroke before he could find her.

I took the bonnet, sent Grandpa back to the house to get the buggy, and followed Grandma's trail on Lightning. When I arrived at the west pasture fence, I found blood sign and a bit of Grandma's dress material hanging on the barbed wire fence. Unable to negotiate the fence line, she had turned south following the barrier. The blood increased my concern. Rather than taking the time to follow the barely visible tracks, I set Lightning into a run. I found her tracks again at the southwest corner. She had worked her way through the fence and turned west on the road that ran south of the pasture.

I had to backtrack east for a quarter of a mile until I could get to a gate. From there it was another flat-out run for two miles on the road until I found her. She was standing in the middle of the road staring into the four o'clock sun. She did not act as if I was present. I stepped down from Lightning and walked toward her. Her face was deep red in color and she was not sweating. She had a small cut on her forearm.

"Grandma, are you all right?"

She didn't look at me but kept staring into the sun. I repeated my question and she mumbled a garbled reply. I took my canteen from the saddle, held her by the arm, and urged her to sit at the edge of the road. I led Lightning to the west of her so she could sit in his shadow. Coaxing her to hold out her hands, palms up, I slowly poured some of the water on her wrists. Bill Sunday had told me that the worst thing a person could do for someone suffering from sunstroke was to pour water on the head.

She showed a response, holding out her hands requesting the canteen. I gave her a small drink and watched her reaction. She seemed to be improving. I soaked her bonnet in water and placed it on her head. She looked at me and showed some signs of recognition.

"How do you feel, Grandma?"

"I've got to find O. C. The chickens are gone."

"What chickens?"

"I can't find the chickens. Tell O. C. they've been taken."

"I found the chickens, Grandma. They were in the trees."

She seemed to relax.

"Andy, I can't find the chickens. We've got to find Grandpa."

Tears welled up in my eyes. I sat down beside her and put my arm around her shoulder. "Grandma, don't worry about those damned chickens. They'll be all right."

Lightning stamped his forefoot and took a step forward. She looked at the pony and smiled. "He's such a nice colt. I told your Grandpa and Bill that they should give the pony to you. You play with him every day, don't you?"

"Yes, Grandma. I play with him every day."

"We ought to find your grandpa. Someone's taken the chickens."

My heart was breaking. All I could do was sit beside her and fight off my tears. She just couldn't seem to get a grip on reality. I don't know how long we sat together on the roadside in silence. The sun was nearly down when I heard Grandpa driving the buggy down the road. When he pulled up, his face was ashen. I helped Grandma to her feet and we gently coaxed her into the buggy. She said nothing as she relaxed in the seat and adjusted her bonnet.

"What happened?" Grandpa asked.

"She said she was looking for the chickens. She said someone took them."

Grandpa's eyes filled with tears. "Chickens! Can you imagine such a thing?"

Grandpa turned without another word and climbed into the buggy next to her. She took hold of his sleeve and adjusted her bonnet with her other hand.

"Where are we going, O. C.?" she asked with a smile.

"We're going home," Grandpa said as he turned the buggy around.

I watched them drive away before I gathered Lightning and lifted myself into the saddle. I felt as if the weight of the world had suddenly settled on my shoulders. I was in no hurry to catch up, choosing to ride through the pasture rather than taking the road back to the house. I just couldn't bring myself to be with them. I needed to be alone and sort through my thoughts.

As I topped a large sandhill, I held up Lightning and dismounted. The last rays of the sun were disappearing to the west behind my back. The farm buildings seemed to glow against the dark sky behind them. Everything looked so normal and beautiful. Horses were circling in the corrals, cattle were walking to the windmill tank for an evening drink of water, and turkeys were roosting in the trees by the pigpens. Laddie was barking at something. I smiled, figuring that he was probably tormenting some cat by the washhouse.

As the sun continued to settle, I could make out lights through the west windows of the house. I needed to get down there and help Grandpa with supper. I had chores to do. I hated milking cows in the dark. Lightning stamped his hoof in the sand. He was eager to get to the barn.

I remembered Grandma standing in the kitchen fixing pies when I was small. I thought of those early mornings when she was in the flowerbed silently working to make that year's garden more beautiful than before. I remembered her smiles and quiet laughter. I thought of the day that Bill brought Lightning and how calmly she reacted to the tiny colt's antics on the porch as she tried to get him to take some milk from the bottle. I remembered those times late in the evening when she could be found rocking on the porch next to Grandpa.

I smiled at the memories before considering what had happened that day. I was going to lose my Grandma. She was going to die and there was nothing I could do about it except help out with her care. Living with so much livestock, new life and death had been a constant cycle throughout my life. We never thought too much about it when one of the animals grew old and died; that was natural and expected. Sometimes, when a newborn foal or calf died, things got pretty discouraging, but that was the way things were and we lived with it.

Now it was Grandma's time to go, but I would always have the memories. She would always be in my thoughts as long as I existed, and she would be as young and well as I chose to remember. At least I had that and nothing could take it.

It was well after dark by the time I finished chores. As I stepped into the house, Grandpa was sitting alone at the kitchen table. The galvanized bathtub was half full of soapy water in the middle of the kitchen floor. He was staring into the lamplight.

"How's Grandma?" I asked.

"I gave her a bath and put her to bed. She went right off to sleep. Your supper is on the stove."

I found my plate and sat across from him at the table. He looked very old that night in the flickering shadows of the oil lamplight. "I'm going to St. John in the morning. I've got to find someone to help us. I want you to stay around the house and make sure she's all right while I'm gone."

"How long will you be gone?"

Grandpa cut his eyes toward me and cast a glum, hollow expression of determination. "As long as it takes."

"Maybe Aunt Jean can help."

"I hope so." Tears welled up in Grandpa's eyes. "I don't know what else to do. We can't have this happen again. I wish I could watch her myself, but we've just got too much to take care of. She's going to need someone full time to see to her needs and take care of her. I've thought of my sister, Liddie. Maybe she could fill in until I could get someone permanent."

I nodded. I hadn't thought of Aunt Liddie but she was an excellent choice. She was a widow and probably could do it, at least for a while. I always liked Liddie. I had stayed with her once when I was eight and helped her pick cherries.

"Try to do the chores early, Andy. Spend the rest of the day around the house. I don't want her near the kitchen or the stove alone. I'm afraid she'll burn herself, or cut herself, or wander off again. We've some harness that needs mending. You could do that."

"Sure, Grandpa. I can do that."

"I wish the Lord had saw fit to take her suddenly. You know...without the suffering. I'm afraid she's going to suffer."

"Maybe it won't be too bad." There was really little else to say. I was afraid of the same thing.

Grandpa rose from his chair. "Maybe not. We can hope it won't be too bad for her."

I watched him make his way toward the bedroom. I could see that same weight that I had felt bearing down upon his shoulders. After a moment I heard the bedroom door close. It was my turn to stare into the small flame of the lantern.

Aunt Liddie stayed with Grandma until a woman named Ester Finch was hired as a housekeeper and nurse. Mrs. Finch was pleasant enough and seemed to get on well with Grandma. She was an attractive widow in her mid-fifties. As Grandma's condition steadily deteriorated over a six-month period, problems began to develop. Grandma became a constant concern. She lost all contact with reality and had to be changed, bathed, fed, and constantly monitored. Mrs. Finch was not up to the responsibility. Grandma's hair was not properly cared for and there were times that Grandpa suspected that she had not been changed throughout the day. Suspicions were verified when Grandpa entered the house early in the afternoon and saw Mrs. Finch strike Grandma while attempting to tie her in a chair. Mrs. Finch was gone by that evening.

Aunt Liddie was again called upon to provide temporary care but she was not in the best of health herself. Grandpa decided to try to get someone younger. Bill Sunday suggested that perhaps one of Jed Groves's daughters might be willing to take the position. Grandpa wrote a letter to Groves and received a reply that the oldest daughter, June, would be willing to take care of Grandma.

On a cold November 12, 1916, I hitched Lightning to the buggy and set out for Great Bend to meet the train. I was waiting at the station the following day when the train was scheduled to arrive. I was more than a little concerned when Jenny stepped off the train. At first I thought both girls had made the trip from Grand Island and June was just slow. In the two years since I had seen Jenny, she had grown a foot and had certainly filled out in places that were not noticeable before. She was an attractive young woman. She recognized me immediately and approached with smiles and greetings. The explanation for the substitution was simple. A rash of marriages at the Groves' household left Jenny as the only alternative. June had decided at the last minute to elope with a teamster from York. Jane had been married the year before. Jenny reassured me that I didn't need to worry because she knew she could handle the job. She had been doing most of the heavy work around the Groves' place anyway. She could cook, sew, clean, shoot, do carpentry work, shoe horses, work teams in the fields, raise gardens, or anything else as well or better than either of her sisters. She was totally capable of handling any job and she was eager to work for wages. She spent the entire eight-hour ride back to the ranch persuading me.

Grandpa and Liddie were kind but concerned when we arrived. At a solidly built five-foot-nine inches, Jenny was certainly physically able to handle the work. It was just that they didn't know whether a sixteen-year-old was prepared for the challenges of caring for Grandma. Jenny's answer was simple. If they ever felt she couldn't handle the job, she would go home. Until then, she expected them to allow her the opportunity to prove herself. After all, they asked for the help and Jed had sent his last available daughter willingly.

After a brief consultation, Grandpa and Liddie agreed that they would give her a try. With that question settled, our life with Jenny began. She worked like a trooper and ran the house like a railroad yard foreman. She cared for Grandma, baked, cleaned, sewed, fixed meals, and monitored all household activities. She made suggestions for improvement of the farm, crops, gardens, livestock program, and certain poor male personal habits that Grandpa and I had developed. Rather than the quiet nights that Grandpa and I spent reading or just sitting, activities were now filled with conversation, new project proposals, teasing, and laughter. In the spring, a new trellis was built for rose vines, the house received a fresh coat of paint, the gardens were expanded, trees planted, the chicken flock expanded, and extra rows of sweet corn planted for caning. A new clothesline was installed and a place for muddy-boot storage assigned, all at Jenny's direction.

Old Bill Sunday was having a ball just keeping track of proceedings. More than once he reminded me of his prediction that she would make me walk the straight and narrow. Just as quickly I reminded him that I was not married to the girl and did not expect to be. Besides, she was too young. I was almost six years older—a vast age and maturity gap. We were also related. After all, her father was my grandpa's second cousin. I had my eye on a girl in Seward named Lucy Bowden. She was the daughter of a prosperous farmer and much sweeter.

But what I told Bill Sunday and thought to myself were two different stories. After being around Jenny, Lucy Bowden was boring. Jenny always had something to talk about. Lucy seemed dull-witted by comparison. Lucy was pretty, but Jenny was prettier and interesting to boot—although her constant defense of the Democrats and President Wilson didn't sit well in the house. After all, everyone knew that the greatest president that ever lived was Theodore Roosevelt. It was Roosevelt who carried the big stick and the Republican Party that provided high farm prices for the country by staying out of the war. All Wilson could talk about was income tax and international involvement. Other than that one shortcoming, I thought a great deal of Jenny. She was honest, forthright, hardworking, and dependable. Her personality was funny, clever, and outgoing.

It was Jenny's care of Grandma that most impressed me. Grandma's condition demanded almost constant attention. By mid-summer she was totally bed-ridden. Taking care of her was a staggering responsibility. In spite of Jenny's attentions, Grandma drifted ever deeper into a sea of darkness. By fall sores were developing on her back, and no matter what Jenny tried to do, they grew worse. The doctor diagnosed the sores as a cancer. He figured Grandma was full of it. Grandma lasted through the winter but passed on two days before Easter.

I was hitching a team in front of the barn when Grandpa walked from the house. He was sad, but he seemed to move more smoothly than he had in months. It seemed as though the burden he had been carrying had been lifted.

"Grandma's gone," he stated bluntly.

In spite of the fact that I knew it was coming, I felt like a mule had kicked me in the stomach. I leaned forward and placed my head on the back of the mule I was hitching to the team. I was hurt that we had lost her, but relieved that she didn't have to suffer anymore.

"Don't let it affect you that way," Grandpa said. "It's for the best. I know she's happier. That cancer was eating her up. She's got to be in a better place."

"I know that. I'll just miss her."

"She's been gone for some time, Andy. That wasn't her in that bed. It was just her body."

He then turned away and went for a walk in the pasture. I believe he took Grandma with him for one last visit.

We buried Grandma in the Eden Valley Community Cemetery. One fellow counted over two hundred buggies and wagons in her funeral procession. We used Lightning to pull our buggy at Grandpa's insistence. The preacher gave a sermon about mothers and what the Bible teaches about them. He also stated that if the meek and good would inherit the earth, Nell Tate would be first in line for the rewards.

Although there were tears, my feelings weren't the same as they had been the day we had searched for Grandma when she wandered off. I had already said my good-byes long before.

Grandpa asked Jenny to stay on with us. He said the house would be lonely without her. I gave brief thought of approaching Grandpa about going off on my own, but decided against it. Jenny was the reason. She had become a good friend and a part of the family. Although we were friends, I didn't know how she would feel about the idea of courting. I finally found the opportunity when I learned of a dance to be held in Seward. I stewed over the decision the entire night before, mustering the courage. My problem was that I didn't know how to dance. I had never been on a dance floor in my life. If she accepted the invitation, I didn't know what she would do when we got there and all I could do was stand around stupidly and watch her dance with other guys.

We were eating our breakfast when I finally mustered the courage to ask. I blurted the invitation in the middle of the meal, totally changing the conversation. Both of them stared at me like they had been assaulted. I felt stupid and awkward. After her initial shock, Jenny smiled and nodded.

That Saturday night, I hitched Lightning to the buggy and drove it up to the house. I couldn't believe it when Jenny stepped from the porch door. She was wearing a fine purple dress. A matching purple hat made her look like one of those Gibson girls in the magazines. I helped her into the buggy and we set off to Seward.

We made small talk for a while before Jenny presented her confession. She didn't know how to dance. I immediately consoled her, confessing that I didn't know how to dance either.

"Then why are we going to a dance?" Jenny asked.

"Because I wanted to take you out," I answered honestly. It seemed the best course of action.

"What are we going to do? Just stand around?"

"No, I thought we would dance."

"How?"

"It can't be that difficult—certainly no worse than learning to ride a horse. I figured we'd learn together."

A sudden gleam came to her eye. "Why not?"

I urged Lightning forward. All my fears vanished and I was eager to learn to dance with Jenny.

When we stepped into the hall—her in her fanciest purple dress and me in my store-bought suit—we saw everyone else dressed in work clothes, swinging their partners, do-si-do-ing, alman left-ing, and cutting up a storm.

I looked toward Jenny with a feeling of embarrassed wonderment. She only laughed and removed her hat.

"I'd a lot rather learn this kind of dancing, anyhow. Wouldn't you?"

"Sure would!" I slipped off my coat, loosened my tie, and led my partner to the dance floor. By the end of the evening we were old pros at the social art of square dancing.

As we made our way home, I stopped the buggy to allow Lightning a breather. There was only a quarter moon, but the stars filled the sky. Out there on the open prairie, under that canopy of stars, it felt like we were the only people in the world. We sat in silence for quite a while.

"Mama says she'd rather I waited until I was eighteen."

"For what?"

"But, I'll be seventeen in February."

"You will?"

"Sometimes you're the slowest person in the world. If I had to wait for you to ask me, I'd probably die an old maid!"

"Would you?"

"Would I what?"

My throat was so tight I thought I was going to choke. "Marry me."

"Finally! Yes, Andy, I'll marry you."

For several moments I didn't know what to do. I thought about urging Lightning forward. I wondered if I should say "thank you." I considered jumping from the buggy and running for my life.

"I would think it would be all right for you to kiss me, if you wanted to," she said softly.

That suggestion sounded like a reasonable alternative to any of my plans. So I did.

Grandpa was quite pleased when we informed him of our decision over breakfast the following morning. He asked us what we intended to do after we were married. Neither of us had given the matter much thought. He offered us a full partnership in the ranch, stating that there was more than enough work for all and that he was getting to an age where it wouldn't be long before he simply would not be able to handle the physical challenges of maintaining the place alone. He also surprised us with the news that he had already consulted my aunts and uncles about the partnership during Grandma's funeral. They had agreed and the family was waiting for Jenny and me to get on with it.

We were married at Eden Valley Community Church on Jenny's birthday, February 11, 1917. It was a small service with only close family and friends attending. Jenny's parents were unable to attend because of the distance, but insisted that we spend some time with them at our earliest convenience. Her mother also sent her wedding dress for the occasion. Our honeymoon consisted of a weekend trip to Great Bend. Lightning pulled the buggy. We returned to the ranch the following Monday. In those days there wasn't the luxury of long absences or vacations. Ranch chores and responsibilities made it impossible for us to be gone any longer. Livestock needed care and feeding during the winter. Calving season usually began the last week of February and we had several first-calf heifers demanding constant monitoring.

It was the third week of March when a spring blizzard roared in from the north. Heavy snow, accompanied by violent winds, began falling in the late afternoon. After a brief family conference concerning our options, Grandpa gathered stock into the barn stalls and I saddled Lightning to bring in the cattle and small calves into the corrals. Small calves, especially newborns, often suffocate in snowdrifts. It seemed a simple task, but none of us imagined the ferocity that this storm held. Grandpa insisted that I wear a heavy buffalo robe coat of his in case of trouble. That old coat weighed at least thirty pounds, but it could provide warmth in the worst of weather.

Before I reached the far end of the pastures a blinding onslaught of snow and wind engulfed me. I wrapped a bandana around my mouth and ears for added protection and pulled the heavy collar of the coat up to my neck.

I found a cow trying to give birth on the downwind side of a steep hill. She was down and the calf's badly swollen nose and tongue were exposed at the opening of the birth canal. There was no sign of the calf's front feet. I needed to help with the birth. I had to push the calf's head back into the birth canal and adjust the position of the feet. I dreaded removing my coat and rolling up my shirtsleeves in the midst of a blizzard, but there was nothing else to do if I wanted to save the cow.

The cow was already weak from straining and did not resist my efforts. I had to push the calf back in as far as my arm could reach, then locate the feet and start them through. I had to move fast because the placenta had already ruptured, exposing the calf's face, and the calf would drown within minutes. The problem with the maneuver was that the cow continued to strain and the pressure upon my arm was painful. It took patience to locate the feet and pull them into position, one leg at a time.

As snow pounded against my face and cold ripped through my chest and exposed left arm, I found the feet quickly and started them through. The calf's head had swollen so badly that I had to help with the birth by pulling on the calf. With feet still slick from birth fluid, it was difficult to pull the calf with bare hands. Once the feet were out, I slipped the noose of my lariat around them and tried to pull in time with the cow's straining. It was no use as there simply wasn't enough room left for the swollen head. After a few attempts, the calf came through. I cleaned the mouth of debris and fluids. He was a large bull calf but his tongue was so swollen that he couldn't breath. I spun him by his back legs in a circle to clear the breathing passage. He took a breath. I placed the calf beside his mother's head so she could recognize him.

Within minutes she was on her feet, licking the calf clean and urging it to stand, but in the raging storm, the calf was freezing in spite of her efforts. I helped rub the calf clean and heaved it into the saddle, knowing that the cow would follow us into the corrals. By the time I had gathered the calf and cow it was growing dark and I could see no more than a few yards as the snow and ice pelted me from all directions. Nightfall found me hopelessly lost in the rolling maze of sandhills.

Realizing that the cow would be unable to follow, I returned the calf to her, hoping they could survive on their own. For the first time in my life, I feared for my life. If I didn't get back to the protection of the farmstead quickly, I knew I would freeze to death.

I gave Lightning his head, hoping he would know the way back to the barns. I could feel the cold penetrating into me. I struggled to maintain consciousness.

It seemed like hours as the pony struggled through the darkness. I was concerned that we were going in circles. I thought of sleeping in the saddle but knew that the urge to sleep was the first sign of freezing.

Lightning stopped. I urged him forward but he refused to move. I was afraid; he was my last hope of making it back. I dismounted to lead him. Perhaps if I kept moving I wouldn't freeze. I took two steps and walked right into the side of a building. I was standing against the wall of the barn. I worked my way along the wall, searching for a doorway. I soon found a sliding door but it was frozen solid. I worked my way further to the north to the west walk-in door and knocked the ice loose from the door latch. The latch freed and I swung the door open, leading Lightning inside.

I fumbled down the central alleyway until I found the end stall. We kept a kerosene lantern hanging there for late-night milking and checking stock. I opened the great coat and fished a match from my vest pocket.

In the dim glow of the lantern light, the interior of the barn took on the bizarre appearance of an ice cave as fine snow filtered through the walls and coated itself throughout the interior. Lightning's nose and eyes were coated with a layer of ice and snow. I wondered how long he could have continued. I wiped his nose and eyes clear and gave him a hug around the neck. After putting Lightning into his stall and giving him a large ration of grain and hay, I briefly considered trying to walk to the house. It was at least a hundred yards and I couldn't see a foot. I had heard stories of the old days when men had frozen to death within a few feet of a house in a blizzard. I crawled into a pile of loose hay, wrapped my feet in saddle blankets, drew the heavy buffalo coat closely about me, and settled in for a long night.

Jenny's voice woke me. As I opened my eyes, I saw her grim expression of concern. Grandpa was standing behind her, holding a lantern.

"What time is it?" I asked.

"It must be around four. When the storm broke a bit and we could see the barn, we came out to see if you had made it back."

"I almost didn't. I thought I was a goner there for a while. If it hadn't been for Lightning, I would have lost my way."

"We need to get back to the house as soon as possible," Grandpa said. "The wind could rise again at any moment and I would just as soon spend the rest of this storm in the house."

It wasn't long after we had settled in the kitchen for some warming coffee that the wind increased. The blizzard continued for most of the following day. When it cleared, the buildings were surrounded by snowdrifts to the eaves. We lost eight calves in the storm. I didn't find the newborn bull calf of that night until after the snow thawed. Although she had survived the storm, his mother had not been able to save him. We marketed several short-eared and bob-tailed calves that year. Thanks to Lightning, the worst injury I had from the cold was a frostbitten big toe on my left foot that took most of the spring to heal.

We took on a contract to break one hundred mules for the French government that spring for the war effort in Europe. Bill Sunday was a partner in the venture and we hired some Larned men to help. With our regular farm work and the contract, we put in many long days. To add to the pressure, Grandpa was kicked in the leg and was laid up for several weeks. One of the Larned men broke an arm struggling with a mule in the breaking corral.

Cooking for five men that spring kept Jenny busy. The potential profits kept us working hard in hopes of buying more land if everything worked out. The contract was substantial and we cleared several thousand dollars.

Certain jobs were neglected. We had only been able to patch up our fences from the damage of the blizzard instead of a thorough repair. By mid-summer we were having trouble with stock getting into the crops. It was mid-July when Bill Sunday requested my help gathering some stray cows. Bill had a wild half-Longhorn. We had to rope her to get her back to Bill's home range. Grandpa was not fully healed from the mule kick, so it was up to Bill and me to get the cow alone.

We found that old Longhorn hiding in some scrub thickets ten miles east of Bill's place. She was in no mood to return peaceably. I was riding Lightning and Bill was using his best roper, a sorrel mare named Trixie. Once I was able to drive the Longhorn from the thickets, she took off at a full run. The moment we would get into range, she would cut away or turn back on us. We decided to haze her from both sides. She made her way into a grove of catalpa trees and I almost lost my head in a collision with a low-hanging branch. We drove her from the grove across open grassland. Bill and I swung our horses in behind at a full run. Just as we were closing in, Trixie put her foot into a gofer hole and crashed nose-first into the sand, flipping head-over-heels. Bill was caught in his saddle and was bent backward over the high cantle. I could hear bones breaking as they crashed into the ground.

Trixie's front right leg was broken in half. As she thrashed in agony, Bill hung in the saddle like a rag doll. I jumped from the saddle and tried to settle the frantic mare. Bill's eyes were open but his mouth was full of dirt. His arms hung loosely to his sides. I threw my weight on Trixie's neck to hold her and tried to talk Bill into getting free from the saddle. Although he was conscious and could hear what I was saying, he was simply hurt too badly to move. His Colt and holster were slung in front of him. I crawled from the mare's neck and pulled the pistol. As the mare tried to gain her footing, I placed the muzzle of the barrel against her ear and pulled the trigger.

I reached into Bill's mouth with my fingers and raked out the lodged dirt. He took a deep breath and coughed up blood. I tried to drag him free from under the horse but he only groaned in pain. I had to leave him on his side, his left leg under the mare. I retrieved my canteen and soaked my bandana to wash the dirt from Bill's mouth and nose.

As I washed the filth from his face, Bill was able to speak. "Don't move me. I'm all busted up inside. My ribs are crushed, and I think my back may be broke. I couldn't stand it."

I could feel myself shaking uncontrollably. "I've got to do something. I can't leave you like this. It must be fifteen miles to help."

Bright blood oozed from the side of Bill's mouth as he coughed softly. He shook his head weakly. "It's no use. You've got to go. I'll make out all right until you get back."

"God, I hate to do this."

Bill smiled. "I know boy, but you've got no choice. Go...go now."

The Davis place was fifteen miles north but I had no idea if anyone would be home. My best option was to head for the house where I knew there were men and equipment. I swung into the saddle and set Lightning for home at a full run.

No man should push a horse the way I did. With each pounding mile, I unmercifully drove him forward. He was wheezing for breath and lathered throughout when we staggered into the yard. As I stepped from the saddle and ran for the house, I heard him collapse. I was afraid to look back. I knew I had run him to death.

Jenny met me at the door. Her face reflected the fear in my own as I told her of Bill's condition. She gathered sheets and a mattress from one of the beds as I hitched two mules to the buckboard. Grandpa followed her from the house, supporting himself with a cane. As they drove the wagon from the yard, I saddled old Ben. I couldn't tolerate looking toward Lightning lying on his side in the yard.

We found Bill as I left him. As Jenny and I lifted on the mare, Grandpa dragged him free. He lifted Bill into a sitting position as Jenny and I arranged the mattress on the buckboard.

Grandpa offered him some water but he shook his head. He looked up at Grandpa and made an effort to smile. "Hell of a wreck."

"You just be still. We'll get you home directly."

"No use for that. I'll never stand the trip."

"Don't be saying that. You'll make it."

Bill took hold of Grandpa's hand. "Is there any message you have for Nell?"

Grandpa gasped and shook his head. "Just that I love her."

Bill smiled and nodded. He shuddered slightly and a deep rattle came from his chest. His eyes faded but never left the face of his old friend.

Grandpa slowly raised his free hand to close Bill's eyes. Jenny and I waited silently until Grandpa lowered Bill's head back to the ground.

It was sunset when we drove the buckboard into the yard. Lightning was standing by the breaking corral.

We lifted Bill from the wagon and took him into the house where we could clean him up and arrange his final position. I checked Lightning and unsaddled him. I spent an hour currying, graining, and stroking him. Once again I had demanded more than I should have and he had given his all. I decided that I would never work him again. Sunday's colt would live out his days in retirement.

We buried Bill on a sandy knoll west of the house in the shade of a small cottonwood tree. He told Grandpa years before that he didn't want to be planted in some city or church cemetery. Grandpa emptied a small jar of dirt from Bill's cabin over his remains before we closed the grave. It was Texas dirt and was to be placed over him when he went under. Grandpa told the Eden Valley congregation that Bill loved his place in the sandhills of Kansas but wanted a little Texas dirt to comfort him through the ages. I never imagined Bill to be so sentimental.

A lawyer in St. John wrote us a letter informing that Bill had ordered a last will and testament document shortly after Jenny and I were married. Bill's place was left to Jenny and I. He also asked that Lightning be buried next to him. The lawyer wrote that he had never heard of a man requesting that he be buried next to a horse and had advised that it wasn't a proper request, but the eccentric Texan had been firm in his stipulation. The lawyer stated that there would be no mention of the stipulation if we decided against it. In those days there were no laws concerning where a person should be buried, and if Bill Sunday wanted to be buried next to a horse that is exactly what we would do.

The country went to war the following year. We took another contract for mules for the French army and continued with ranch activities. I registered for the draft but was never called to service. Younger, unmarried men filled the county quota.

We had a son the following year and a daughter fourteen months after. Six years later, a second son was born but didn't survive more than a week. Jenny gave birth to a third son two years later.

The world changed greatly after the war. It wasn't long before the demand for horses and mules dwindled, replaced by new-fangled tractors and automobiles. By the time our oldest boy was ready for fieldwork, we used mules only for row crop tillage and hay harvest. A Caterpillar tractor, Baldwin combine, and Model T Ford automobile slowly replaced the teams. Grandpa had the first Baldwin combine in the county.

During the twenties, farm prices fell and we struggled to keep the place going. If oil hadn't been discovered in the west pastures during the thirties, we would have lost the ranch during the Great Depression and Dust Bowl. Wheat that had sold for two dollars a bushel during World War I was worth no more than six cents. Prices for our cattle fell from fifteen cents a pound to three. Great dust storms from the west blocked sun and filtered through the walls of the house during the bad years. Jenny developed the habit of placing the dishes upside down when setting the table so they wouldn't be covered with dust when we ate. There were times when we would leave lanterns burning all day to light the house. The oil production income was sufficient for us to save our place while others all around us failed. Those were sad times and we spent many helpless nights wondering how we were going to survive. The Porters, Thairs, and several other families left for town work, leaving their farms abandoned. For two years I took a job on a public works program grading roads with mules just to have money to send the children to school.

The depression and President Roosevelt's programs also brought positive changes to the farm. We received telephone service and a few years later the Rural Electric Authority was established to supply electricity. We were able to have refrigeration and wringer washing machines. In the evenings we would gather around the radio and listen to broadcasts from Chicago and New York. Just before World War II, we installed an indoor toilet and shower bath in a converted closet of the original house.

We began receiving daily mail delivery. Trips to St. John, Larned, and Great Bend could be made in a matter of minutes rather than hours. Our one-room community school was closed and we sent our children to high school in St. John. We developed the habit of regular Saturday visits to the town grocery for store-bought bread and to the produce stores to market eggs and lard.

Grandpa passed away in his sleep in 1937 at the age of ninety-five. We buried him next to Grandma in the Eden Valley cemetery. He lived a happy and productive life up to the very end.

I kept my oath to Lightning. He lived to a ripe old age. Often, especially when I was troubled, I would visit him in the pasture with my dog, Laddie, offering a treat of sugar or grain. He would always respond to my call and eagerly accept the treat. Unlike his days as a colt, however, he would stand calmly and accept my attentions.

He was grazing on a hilltop in the summer of 1940 when a thunderhead appeared in the northwest. Sometime during the storm's approach, a lightning bolt struck him down just as it had his mother so many years before. I found him the next morning on that hilltop, his final mouthful of grass still clinched between his teeth. I left his grain bucket beside him. I reckon Lightning was thirty years old.

We sent our oldest boy, Glenn, off to war in 1941. He was killed at Iwo Jima while serving in the Marines. Jenny and I retired from the farm in 1960, rented out our land and moved to a new house in St. John. Today, the farmstead is nothing like it was. The old barn was destroyed by a tornado in the '50s and the house burned down in the '70s. The sandhill pastures have been worked under and are now covered with modern circle irrigation systems. Acres of irrigated corn and sorghum grain now grow where once there were only sandhill plumb thickets and rolling grassland. There is no room in the modern world for the quiet pastures of yesterday.

If you should ever find yourself in Kansas and should happen to venture four miles west and five miles south of a sleepy little grain elevator village known as Seward, you will find an unbroken corner of one of the circles of irrigated crop land. At the top of a small sandy knoll is a great cottonwood tree. At the base of the tree is a tiny grave plot enclosed by a modest, unpainted picket fence. Inside the fence is a plain, white marble cross with the engraved name, "Bill Sunday." Beside the cross is the relic of a rusty old grain bucket and a small, gray, marble stone jutting just above the surface of the ground. You may have to wipe away the grass and debris to read the simple inscription, "Lightning."

If you visit in the evening on a pleasant summer's day, don't be disturbed to find a very old and feeble couple visiting there as well. Feel free to stop and introduce yourself. They would love the company and enjoy the chance to retell the story of Sunday's colt.

END